ONLY SPITE

(A Sadie Price FBI Suspense Thriller—Book 5)

Rylie Dark

Rylie Dark

Bestselling author Rylie Dark is author of the SADIE PRICE FBI SUSPENSE THRILLER series, comprising six books (and counting); the MIA NORTH FBI SUSPENSE THRILLER series, comprising six books (and counting); the CARLY SEE FBI SUSPENSE THRILLER, comprising six books (and counting); and the MORGAN STARK FBI SUSPENSE THRILLER, comprising three books (and counting).

An avid reader and lifelong fan of the mystery and thriller genres, Rylie loves to hear from you, so please feel free to visit www.ryliedark.com to learn more and stay in touch.

ISBN: 978-1-0943-9507-4

BOOKS BY RYLIE DARK

SADIE PRICE FBI SUSPENSE THRILLER
ONLY MURDER (Book #1)
ONLY RAGE (Book #2)
ONLY HIS (Book #3)
ONLY ONCE (Book #4)
ONLY SPITE (Book #5)
ONLY MADNESS (Book #6)

MIA NORTH FBI SUSPENSE THRILLER
SEE HER RUN (Book #1)
SEE HER HIDE (Book #2)
SEE HER SCREAM (Book #3)
SEE HER VANISH (Book #4)
SEE HER GONE (Book #5)
SEE HER DEAD (Book #6)

CARLY SEE FBI SUSPENSE THRILLER
NO WAY OUT (Book #1)
NO WAY BACK (Book #2)
NO WAY HOME (Book #3)
NO WAY LEFT (Book #4)
NO WAY UP (Book #5)
NO WAY TO DIE (Book #6)

MORGAN STARK FBI SUSPENSE THRILLER
TOO LATE (Book #1)
TOO CLOSE (Book #2)
TOO FAR GONE (Book #3)

CHAPTER ONE

Neon orange spray paint would show up even in the morning gloom. Cole grinned to himself as they approached the abandoned warehouse at the end of the wharf.

Apart from the creepy feeling of being watched that he was trying to ignore, it was perfect.

Especially at this time of year. With only six hours of daylight at the beginning of February in Anchorage, the mornings were late, and the evenings came in early, giving them the cover of darkness for longer. With the streetlights at this unused end of the wharf giving out barely more than a flicker, the chances of being seen—and therefore caught—were slim.

Which was just as well, because if Cole's mother found out what he was up to instead of being on his way to school for the day, he would be in big trouble. The last time he had been caught doing this, there had been hell to pay.

It was worth it, though. Cole grinned at the other two boys and shook the can that he was gripping in his hand. He had perfected his tag now and he was proud of it. He had spent hours designing it until he was happy with the curve and shape of the letters, ensuring a distinctive style that would be recognized as his.

This was what his parents and teachers didn't understand. Graffiti was *an art.* He had dreams of being a serious graf artist one day, even bigger than that English guy Banksy, adorning walls and buildings with art that actually *meant something.*

His mates didn't really understand either. They just thought it was a bit of fun, a chance to stick two fingers up at the cops and the authorities, and at all the rules they were expected to obey by parents, teachers, society…everyone. Being a teenager was stifling. There were worse things they could be doing than tagging a few abandoned buildings.

But for Cole, this was serious. A way to make his mark on the world, to contribute to a subversive art form that transcended cultural norms of what and where art should be.

He never voiced those thoughts to his friends though. They would just laugh at him and ask if he had been getting high again.

"Cole. Come on, these rafters will be perfect to tag, look." Billy pointed to the large wooden beams overhead at the back of the warehouse. Realizing he had stopped following them and gotten lost in his thoughts, Cole jogged over to his mates, holding up his phone to see properly. They should have brought better lights, he thought, because they could barely see anything just by using their phones. It didn't really matter though; he could do his tag without looking now. With his eyes closed, even.

He reached Billy and the other boy, Jerry, and they shook their cans, ready to start spraying. Jerry started dragging some wooden crates over so they could climb up to the rafters in question. It was a bit dangerous, but they had done worse, climbing over rooftops and even over the school gates during the summer holidays. That had been stupid though; that had been the time Cole had gotten caught.

But this warehouse was perfect. All these bare walls meant Cole could come back on his own and practice the new designs he had been working on in his sketch book.

"Hey, what's that?" Billy said suddenly, pointing upwards. Cole shone the light from his phone in the right direction.

"It looks like a bunch of plastic has been hung there," Billy said, sounding confused. "Like there's something wrapped in it."

Jerry stopped dragging crates and came over, sounding excited. "Maybe it's been hidden here on purpose."

"What, like treasure?" Billy scoffed as Jerry started piling crates on top of each other and then using the wall to climb up. "We're not playing pirates anymore. It's not second grade."

But Jerry wasn't listening. He started jumping around on the crates trying to reach the plastic, nearly tumbling off but not caring.

Cole wanted to tell him to stop. There was something about the bundle of plastic that was making him uncomfortable. It looked vaguely humanoid, like some kind of giant alien chrysalis from a science fiction movie. It reminded him, too, of the art installations at the fancy gallery his mother had taken him to for his birthday, where there had been sculptures made out of plastic and metal.

Jerry gave up jumping and threw his spray paint can at the plastic, hard. It wobbled precariously, and a piece of plastic fell down. Grinning in triumph, Jerry grabbed the now hanging end of the plastic and pulled, and it began to slowly unwind, releasing whatever was in it slowly down toward them.

"Hey, something's dripping on me!" Billy complained, wiping his face. As he spoke, a fat drop of liquid landed on Cole's hand and he squinted at it, then recoiled in shock.

It was blood.

He raised his face to the thing lowering toward them with a dawning horror, and as the plastic slowly unraveled, he saw the pale face of a woman staring back at him.

In spite of the waxy appearance of her skin, Cole knew this was no sculpture.

The three boys screamed in unison as the corpse landed with a thump on the floor and the plastic burst, spraying them with blood.

CHAPTER TWO

Fifteen years she had been waiting for the clue that would solve her sister's murder. She felt as though she couldn't stand another minute.

Sadie clambered to the top of the rock that overlooked the river's headwaters, feeling frustration welling up within her.

"There's nothing here to see," she yelled down to Sheriff Cooper, who was exploring around the bottom of the rocky outcrop. She could hear the bitter disappointment in her own voice. She could also hear Cooper splashing about in the river below and hoped he didn't alert any nearby bears to their presence. This was one of their main feeding grounds.

It had been that knowledge that had led them here. The crude map that had been drawn by her dying father's shaky hand hadn't given them much to go on other than a few vague squiggles of trees and mountains, which could have been anywhere in the wilderness around Anchorage. It was only when she had managed to decipher a cluster of smudges as being, in fact, a bear paw, that they had been able to decipher the location of the X next to it.

Or at least, she thought they had. With the bear paw indicating the headwaters, they had both assumed from the rest of the drawing that the X indicated the large outcrop that overlooked the feeding grounds. There was nothing else here but the river, pine trees, and mountains. Nothing else that stood out.

But there was nothing here on the outcrop either, and Sadie wondered if they had misread her father's map completely. If that was the case, then they were back at square one.

And then she would never find out who had killed her sister.

"Sadie!" Cooper's voice cut through her dark thoughts of the past. "Come back down, I think I've found something!"

Feeling renewed hope, Sadie clambered back down the rock and splashed through the river to join Cooper, who was wedged behind a rocky ledge.

"What are you doing?" Sadie asked, bemused.

"There's an opening here," Cooper called to her, and she could hear the echo from his voice. "It's a squeeze to get to so it's easily missed, but it looks as though it opens out into a cave of some kind."

Sadie felt a rush of excitement at his words. This had to be it. It had to be the X.

But why? What was in there? Sadie hesitated for a moment, torn between needing to know what her father was trying to show her, and wondering what fresh horrors could await.

Another body?

But how would her father know about it, if so? Unless…

The possibility that it had been her father all along who had killed her sister, a possibility that she had barely dared to entertain until this moment, bloomed in her mind. Her father had been a mean bastard, especially after her mother's death, and as his drinking had progressed, he had grown meaner still.

Yet Jessica had been his favorite, hadn't she? It was always Sadie rather than her older sister who bore the brunt of her father's fists. But then, it had always been Sadie rather than her older sister who had stood up to him. Jessica had been the peacemaker, and the one who soothed Sadie's bumps and bruises after another beating. She was the one who behaved at school and caused no trouble. *"Why can't you be more like your sister?"* had been her father's favorite refrain.

Sensing her hesitation, Cooper wriggled out from behind the ledge and turned to her, his hand outstretched. "Are you okay? I'm sorry, I know this is a big moment for you. We can take a breather before we go on. Maybe even come back another day?"

His eyes were kind, full of genuine concern for her, and Sadie felt a rush of affection for him in spite of the situation. Less than an hour before, they had shared their first kiss in Cooper's snowcat after weeks of tiptoeing around each other, neither daring to voice their feelings for another. It was a complication that Sadie didn't need, but once it had happened it had felt inevitable.

She shook her head. "I've spent fifteen years waiting to find out what the hell happened to Jessica. I can't keep waiting. Let's go in."

But just as she finished speaking, her cell phone rang. Her work phone. It wasn't Cooper, which meant the call could only be coming from the Anchorage FBI Field Office, and therefore her boss, ASAC Paul Golightly. Turning away from Cooper, Sadie answered her phone impatiently.

"Agent Price," she snapped.

As anticipated, Golightly's gruff tones answered her, dispensing with niceties as usual.

"I need you in Anchorage. Up at the wharf. There's a body been found. Agent O'Hara will meet you there."

Sadie suppressed a sigh. "Can't O'Hara tackle this one on his own?" she asked. She had partnered with O'Hara just a fortnight before on a case up in Prudhoe Bay, and although he was a newly qualified agent, he was sharp.

"I need you," Golightly said, and Sadie felt her stomach sink as she picked up on his tone. This wasn't an average murder—if there could ever be such a thing—but something that required her particular expertise. As a Behavioral Analysis Unit special agent, Sadie was called out to anything that looked as though it might require a knowledge of the darkest impulses of human nature.

Serial killers were her usual specialty.

"Go on," Sadie said, waiting for him to explain.

"The body of a young woman was found wrapped in plastic and hanging from the rafters of one of the old industrial warehouses," the ASAC told her.

"Wrapped in plastic? And then just dumped?" That was odd, Sadie thought, her mind already whirling through various scenarios.

"There was another body like this found last year, before you transferred up here," Golightly went on, and Sadie understood why he was calling her. "Exactly the same. But we couldn't get a lead on the case."

"I'm on my way," Sadie said, ending the call. She turned to Cooper, who looked as disappointed as she was, although part of her was also now gearing up to investigate the body in the warehouse, her adrenaline fizzing. She looked from Cooper to the cave, feeling torn.

"Trouble?"

Sadie nodded. "You might want to keep your radio on," she said. "There's a potential serial killer on the loose in Anchorage."

Cooper's eyebrows flew up his forehead and his face drained of color at the thought. After all, it hadn't been so long since the last one. But he simply nodded, as practical as ever.

"Come on. I'll get you back to the saloon so you can pick up your truck."

Sadie took a last, lingering look at the cave, which almost seemed to be beckoning her now. The key to her family's secrets and the murder of her beloved sister, which had haunted her for years, could be just feet away. She was so close…

She could feel Cooper staring at her, and she sighed as she turned away from the cave.

"As soon as you can, I'll bring you back," he promised.

Sadie nodded, reaching out a hand to touch the cool rock as though bidding it farewell. Whatever secrets it held, they could keep for now.

She swallowed her frustration.

She had a crime scene to get to.

CHAPTER THREE

Getting used to often horribly mutilated bodies was one of the hardest things for a new agent. As Agent O'Hara met her on the wharf, she could see he was fighting to hide his revulsion at the crime scene. She had seen that look on too many agents' faces not to recognize it when she saw it.

She also knew not to mention it.

"Are local police at the scene?" Sadie asked as he led her along the wharf.

O'Hara nodded. "The police chief is there, and a detective, who I think will be working alongside us. He doesn't seem over-friendly."

Sadie grimaced. Working with local law enforcement could always be tricky when you were FBI, as in her experience they often resented the intrusion on what they saw as their turf. When Sadie had arrived back in Alaska and been assigned a case up at the Lynx Lakes, Sheriff Cooper had been much the same toward her, as had his sister, Jane, the deputy.

Obviously, things had changed.

But a serial killer, if that's what this turned out to be, targeting the center of Anchorage could cause plenty of jurisdiction problems, as not only would she cross paths with the local detectives but also Cooper himself, since as county sheriff, he could well end up involved too, especially if bodies started turning up outside the city center.

There was no time to worry about potential conflicts now, though. Right now, she needed to get a look at the body.

The smell of death hit her as soon as she entered the warehouse, but it didn't faze her. She had grown used to it over the years.

Two forensics experts were already going through the warehouse, gathering evidence, while two men stood by the body. One, a middle-aged guy with neat salt-and-pepper hair and keen brown eyes, came over to shake their hands. The police chief.

"Special Agent Price. Agent O'Hara. Thank you for coming."

"Better late than never," the other man said. He was around the same age as the chief, but looked more weathered, lean and wiry with a downturned mouth and bushy gray eyebrows. His dark eyes swept over Sadie disdainfully. She met them with a cool gaze, wondering if his hostility was due to the fact that she was a Fed or the fact that she was both a Fed and a woman. She had met enough old-school, misogynistic detectives who thought women should be nowhere near a crime scene in her time, to not recognize when she was in the presence of one.

"This is Detective Linden," the chief said, almost apologetically. "I want you to work closely together on this case."

Sadie nodded at the detective, who, unlike his superior, made no attempt to shake their hands. She suppressed a sigh, and the sinking feeling that this case was going to be harder than it needed to be. Then she turned her attention to the body.

It was a young woman with long, pale hair, and Sadie's eyes swept over the girl's frozen, terrified features, forcing herself to look. To remind herself that a victim was never just "the body." They were people, with hopes and dreams for the future that would never be realized thanks to a cold-blooded killer. Sadie knew that many agents couldn't allow themselves to humanize the victims too much; that it was too painful and keeping a dispassionate view was the safest way to operate. But personally, Sadie found that the pain motivated her.

It made her angry, and that made her determined to find the killer, at all costs.

It was an attitude that had nearly gotten her killed on more than one occasion, but it was also why she had such a good track record of cracking high-profile and complicated cases. If there was a suspected serial killer in Alaska, she knew she would be the first agent assigned to the case. If that sometimes felt more like a burden than a source of pride, then it was one that she had taken on herself.

Detective Linden's attitude didn't matter. This woman did.

"What do we know so far?" Sadie asked the police chief.

"There's nothing to identify the victim," he told her, "so we will have to wait for DNA and fingerprints—or a missing person's report. As you can see, her hands and feet are bound, and the coroner's report may reveal more, but it looks as though there's just the one wound, a slice to the abdomen."

Sadie winced as the implications of that hit her. She was carefully avoiding looking at Agent O'Hara, who hadn't yet seen enough bodies to be able to entirely subdue his reactions. She was aware of him though, standing stiffly next to her, looking anywhere but at the victim.

"So, she bled out while wrapped in the plastic?" *Or suffocated first*, she added silently, wondering what kind of sick mind would condemn a young woman to such a terrifying fate.

The chief nodded. "Yeah. Some teenagers cutting school found her and got her down, not knowing what was in there. The body was completely encased. When it landed blood went everywhere as you can see. Kids were terrified."

"I bet," Sadie murmured. She knelt down near the body, careful not to disturb anything, her eyes sweeping over the scene. Taking in the woman's delicate features and slim frame, wondering why she had been targeted. Was she known to the killer, or did she fit a particular profile? Of course, sometimes being a female alone was enough. Women made up the majority of victims of serial killers, assuming from what Golightly had told her that that's what this was, and the majority of serial killers were men. It was one of the things that made the violence of serial killers stand out against other forms of homicide, where the victims were predominantly men, and often men from marginalized communities.

This woman, however, could have been simply in the wrong place at the wrong time, managing to attract the attention of a monster.

What had been her last movements, that brought her here to a disused warehouse and a plastic tomb?

Until they knew who she was, Sadie knew those questions would go unanswered.

And maybe even then. Thoughts of Jessica, whose cold case had been her top priority just an hour before, came to mind and for once, Sadie allowed them in. Since her arrival back in Alaska she had come to terms with the fact that it was largely her sister's unsolved death that motivated her. That she had turned her grief and pain into a need to find justice for victims and understand those who preyed on them, only enough to bring them in.

Sadie wrinkled her nose as a strong smell hit her that she knew instantly. She turned her head toward O'Hara, who had stepped up behind her but stayed standing, no doubt not wanting to get too close.

"Can you smell that, O'Hara?"

His pallor looked sickly under the light of their flashlights, but his expression was carefully neutral. He nodded.

"It smells like the harbor," he said. "Sea and fish."

Sadie straightened up. "That's what I thought. So, she was kept on a boat maybe, or the plastic comes from one." She looked at the chief again. "This is all the same as the first case?"

It was Detective Linden who answered her. "Yeah," he said in a hoarse voice that had known too much tobacco, "the MO is exactly the same. First victim was a local college student, but an out-of-towner. New to the area."

Sadie nodded, suspecting this current victim would fit much the same profile, given her likely age. If someone was picking off college students, then that gave them a place to start.

"There were no leads?" she asked and was surprised when Detective Linden openly glared at her. It must have been his case, she realized, and if he was anything like her, he would be cursing that he wasn't able to solve it.

"No," he said, and she could hear the anger in his voice. "I had a team on it day and night, but we found nothing."

And now there was another body.

Linden's tone almost seemed to be daring Sadie to challenge him on his competence. It was obvious the old guy's ego was bruised. She could understand that, but she didn't have time for it. She looked around again, scanning her flashlight around the floor of the warehouse. Bloody drag marks led over toward the forensics team.

"So, she was transported here," she said aloud, but more to herself, organizing her thoughts, "and then hung up while she was potentially still alive." She sensed O'Hara shudder next to her.

"We know all that," Linden retorted. "You're an hour late and a dollar short, honey."

Sadie ignored him, although she felt herself bristle at the "honey." She was right, she thought, he was a chauvinist. Well, he was going to have to get used to being led by a woman, because if this turned out to be a serial, then this was *her* case. And she wasn't going to let Linden distract her from what she needed to do.

She shone her flashlight in wider, concentric circles, stopping at a pair of smeared boot prints in the drag marks.

"Forensics will run those prints," she said to O'Hara, "but it's likely nothing to get too excited about, unless our guy was wearing a particularly rare brand of footwear." She continued shining her flashlight around the warehouse. Forensics knew what they were doing, but things could sometimes be missed. She could sense Linden watching her.

Then one of the forensics team, a young guy with a neat beard who was at the other side of the warehouse, gave them a shout.

"There are a few partial footprints over here," he said, sounding excited. "They lead out of the back door."

With Linden and O'Hara following, Sadie jogged toward the exit, her adrenaline rising.

CHAPTER FOUR

Recent footprints meant the killer could still be close. Sadie could feel anticipation thudding in her chest as she reached the exit to the warehouse.

Outside the exit, a fire door that was heavy to open, a small stone staircase led down to an alley. A single, partial footprint was evident on the second step. As forensics got to work on it, Sadie carefully sidestepped it and went into the alley, scanning eagerly with her light for any more evidence, but she could see nothing.

"Where does the alley lead?" she asked Linden, who had jogged up behind her. O'Hara was watching the two forensics guys as they took casts of the print and scraped up samples of the dried blood. The killer hadn't been careful enough, Sadie thought. Almost sloppy, in fact.

It was a trait that she had seen before. Pathological narcissism was common in serial killers—practically a requirement, she often thought—and that often led to a sense of superiority, almost a cocky self-assurance that they wouldn't get caught. That led to mistakes being made.

Perversely, some killers almost *wanted* to be caught, at least after they had accumulated so many bodies. There was a notoriety and infamy to being a serial killer that could make some of them darker versions of celebrities. Sadie knew that there were people who would pay a small fortune online for serial killer memorabilia, and who clamored for the chance to write to them in prison.

Hell, there were even women who wanted to marry them. Sadie figured that if you were a pathological killer, then getting caught in a high-profile case as a notorious serial in a state that didn't have a death penalty might not seem such a bad idea.

And any killer with infamy as a partial motivation would need more than two bodies, Sadie thought. Which meant, if they didn't catch this guy, there would be more.

She could almost feel sorry for Detective Linden, knowing that if she had been unable to solve a case only for another victim to turn up six months later, the horror of that would be keeping her awake at night.

"More alleyways," Linden replied. "They don't lead to anything much, just wasteland. There's a small community of the homeless around; they might have seen something. The alleys fork at the end of this one, so we should split up."

There was a note of authority in his tone, but this wasn't the time to challenge it. Sadie nodded. "Okay. Agent O'Hara and I will go right. We can meet back here."

She walked off without looking at Linden, her focus purely on the task at hand, taking a right at the end of the alleyway into another, narrower one. O'Hara jogged behind her to catch up.

"He's a grumpy old coot," the younger agent murmured. "Didn't even acknowledge my existence."

"He'll thaw out," Sadie said, although she suspected that was wishful thinking. "Just try not to rise to him if he offends you. Remember why we're here."

O'Hara nodded, looking around him as Sadie shone her flashlight around the alleyway, but there were no more footprints or drag marks, or even any indication that anyone had passed down here recently. Perhaps Linden would have more luck.

Of course, the footprints may not belong to the killer at all, which made her previous musings about this guy's nature moot. Someone else other than the boys who called it in could have come across the body. It seemed unlikely though. How many people spent their time hanging around old warehouses?

As Linden had told her, the alley came out onto a patch of wasteland, scattered with disused, broken machinery and old crates. Patches of old ice cracked underfoot, and the temperature seemed to have dropped suddenly. Sadie was glad for the extra layer of thermals she had on underneath her uniform. In a late Alaskan winter, the more layers the better.

Her reasons for coming back to Alaska had been varied, but the climate certainly wasn't one of them.

"There's a fire," O'Hara said, pointing to a light in the distance. They trudged toward it and saw a small camp made up of a few old tents, pieces of tarpaulin and boxes, and a few street people huddled around a barrel fire.

"Can you imagine that?" O'Hara said with barely disguised horror. "Being homeless in this cold?"

Sadie nodded sadly, thinking of the statistics of homeless people who froze to death every winter up and down the States. The world was a cruel place.

But there were moments of joy in it. The memory of the kiss between herself and Sheriff Cooper that morning made her cheeks suddenly flush, and the pit of her belly tighten. She shook her head as if to dislodge the thought. She couldn't afford to be distracted by whatever was going on between her and Cooper.

As they approached the fire, the five figures huddled around it stiffened instantly. Wary eyes watched them, peering out of bundles of old clothes and torn, dirty blankets. She doubted they would get anything useful out of the group; homeless people inevitably had more reason than most to be distrustful of anyone in authority, and wary of disclosing anything that could potentially be used against them. But at the same time, they were often in a position to notice things that other people didn't, precisely because the majority of society didn't notice *them.* The homeless were often treated as though they were invisible, and invisible people could go where others couldn't.

Detective Linden, as a local, might have more luck here, she thought. Potentially even a few informants.

Still, they were here, so they had to try.

Trying to keep her body language as non-threatening as possible, Sadie flashed her badge.

"Special Agent Price, FBI," she said quietly. At her words, a man and woman looked across the fire at each other and slunk off away into the darkness. The others, two men and an elderly woman, remained, three pairs of intensely distrustful eyes shining in the firelight.

"What do you want with us?" one of the men, who seemed to be in charge of the fire, almost growled at her. The elderly woman, however, looked more curious, peering at Sadie from under her hoodie which was pulled tightly around her face.

"We don't get many visits from the FBI," she said, sounding almost amused. Sadie smiled at her.

"We're investigating an incident up at the warehouses," she told her, while watching the two men, who were listening intently, out of the corner of her eye. She saw them glance at each other quickly. Too quickly.

They knew something.

"It's very serious," she went on, although her voice was calm. Non-threatening. "So I'm just wondering if any of you have seen or heard anything today? Around the industrial estate? Anything that seems out of the ordinary at all?"

There was a silence. The woman seemed to be considering her question, cocking her head to one side like a bird. The man in charge of the fire was openly glaring at them while the other man stared resolutely into the flames as though he had decided to simply pretend they weren't there.

"Anything at all?" Sadie prompted. "Even the smallest things can turn out to be relevant."

"Anything you know could be really helpful," O'Hara added encouragingly. With his fresh-faced, boyish looks, he was perfect for this, Sadie thought. Most people seemed to like O'Hara on sight. The old woman smiled at him in a way that Sadie thought was positively grandmotherly.

"We don't know anything," the man poking the fire snapped, his tone almost menacing. "Leave us alone."

Sadie ignored him and looked at the other two. The other man was still staring into the middle of the flames, seemingly lost deep in his own world now. Maybe he was.

"And the rest of you?" she asked. "This isn't going to cause any trouble for you," she assured them, "I just want to know if you've seen or heard anything that could help us."

There was another long silence, in which the man continued to glare at them, the other to gaze into the fire as though it was a portal to another world, and the old woman to peer at them from under her hood. She had a hooked nose and long chin, and Sadie half expected her to start cackling at any moment.

"Okay," Sadie said eventually. "Thanks for your help."

They walked away, Sadie shining her flashlight around the rest of the wasteland. There was nothing and no one to be seen and she wondered where the other two homeless people had gone. She walked back toward the alley with O'Hara, wondering where Detective Linden was and whether he had discovered anything useful.

"They knew something," O'Hara said as they reached the alleyway. It was growing brighter now, and Sadie turned off her flashlight as she nodded.

"Yeah, thought so too. We need to come back and try and question them without the guy who was tending the fire present. He was stopping the others from speaking."

She had just entered the alleyway when she heard footsteps behind, gaining on them quickly. She whirled around, her hand immediately going to her holster just in case, to see a woman in an old, moth-eaten fur coat. Sadie was sure that it was the woman who had slunk away from the fire as she and O'Hara had approached.

"Agent," she said quickly, in a low tone, looking hurriedly around. Sadie spotted her companion lingering a few feet behind, waiting for her. "You need to look for Scrapper."

"Thank you," Sadie said, grateful for the lead. "Who's Scrapper?"

"He's a mean guy," the woman said. "A thief too. I saw him follow some boys into the estate earlier this morning. Schoolkids. I reckon he was going to try and rob them." She shook her head in disdain. "They were just kids, really, you know? Then he came running out, gabbling something about blood and a body. I asked him what he was talking about, and he said he was getting out of there because the police would be coming. Well, I don't like the police, so I went back to the fire."

"So why are you telling me now?" Sadie asked gently, wondering if the woman had a grudge against this Scrapper guy and was just wasting her time. Her instincts told her that the woman was telling the truth, however. Although her face was lined and she looked desperately thin, her eyes and voice suggested that her sudden informant wasn't much older than the victim, and her guts twisted in empathy, wishing that there was something she could do for her. Society let too many people slip through the cracks with no safety net to catch them.

"Look, I don't know nothing about no body," the woman said, becoming defensive now. "But it's not right, is it, someone going around hurting people like that? Could be one of us, and no one would care." She said the last matter-of-factly, without any self-pity, and Sadie smiled sadly.

"Do you think this Scrapper could have anything to do with it?" she asked the woman, who looked thoughtful and then shrugged.

"Dunno," she said. "He looked like he really was shook up, you know? But like I said, he's mean. He could kill someone."

"Where can we find him?"

The woman looked scared. "You're not going to tell him I told you?"

"I'm not going to mention you at all," Sadie promised. "Do you know where he could be? We just need to ask him what he saw, that's all."

Although Sadie was already wondering just how much this Scrapper guy might know.

"Anywhere along the wharf around here that's not used," the woman said. "People use it as a bit of a dumping ground, and you can find things sometimes that you can use or sell. Scrapper's good at that, that's why we call him that. Don't ask me his real name," she warned, eyeing Sadie warily now. "I don't know it and I wouldn't tell you if I did."

"It's okay," Sadie said. The woman was backing away, having told them either all she could or all that she was willing to. "You've been really helpful."

The woman nodded, and then turned and ran back to her partner. Sadie watched her for a minute and then turned to O'Hara.

"Right," she said. "Let's go and find Scrapper before he disappears. If he thinks the police are looking for him, he'll be away from the wharf faster than we can spit."

They ran back down the alleyway.

CHAPTER FIVE

Sadie could hear nothing but the howling of the wind and O'Hara's boots on the gravel behind her as they made their way slowly along the wharf, eyes peeled for any sign of a man who could be Scrapper.

This end of the wharf was desolate, with nothing but a row of shuttered buildings, many with windows that had been boarded and reboarded, no doubt in an attempt to keep the homeless from seeking shelter, a few with doors hanging off, allowing access to the interior. Like the warehouse where the as yet unnamed victim had been found, covered in plastic and her own blood.

Sadie shuddered and felt the wind blow through her, chilling her very bones.

As they walked past a smaller building with its door replaced by a piece of easily moved corrugated iron, O'Hara paused.

"I can hear something inside," he murmured quietly enough so that Sadie had to lip read.

Really? she mouthed back, impressed by his hearing skills. All she could hear was wind. O'Hara nodded and Sadie motioned for him to move the corrugated iron enough to let them through, which the younger agent did as carefully and quietly as possible. Sadie kept her hand on her holster as she followed him inside to the dark, freezing building, trying to adjust her eyes to the gloom.

Once inside, she heard Scrapper before she saw him, switching on her flashlight. A man was hunched in a corner of the small warehouse, dismantling what looked to be a junction box, yanking out any leftover wiring. He looked at them, his eyes glinting in the light of her flash. He was a small man, wiry, with intelligent black eyes, clothed in a big parka with a fur hood that looked as though it had never been laundered. Perhaps it hadn't.

"Scrapper?" Sadie said slowly. "We need to ask you a few questions."

The man flinched at the mention of his name, his eyes darting from her to O'Hara and back again. "You're cops?"

"FBI," Sadie said. Scrapper's eyes flew open, and he froze in a way that Sadie knew meant he was poised to flee. She had barely finished the thought before the small man darted into the darkness.

"Freeze!" Sadie yelled, but they only heard Scrapper's boots pounding on the warehouse floor. She drew her gun as they raced after him. A fire door clanged shut at the back of the building and she sped up, cursing inwardly. Why had no one secured these old places properly? She heard O'Hara thundering along behind her.

They came out of the fire door on the other side of the wharf where it bent around in an arc before leading up to the quay. Scrapper was already yards ahead, racing toward the quay before suddenly darting down a gap between two outhouses. O'Hara cursed under his breath.

"Damn it, he's fast," he huffed, a few strides behind Sadie. Out of nowhere, she thought of Cooper, who always tried to outrun her, their pride getting the better of them as they both tried to be top dog on a case.

She missed working with him, which was almost strange when some of the most dangerous cases of her career had been recently by Cooper's side. And to think that as a girl growing up, she had thought that Alaska was the most boring place on earth.

It was almost as though she had brought the trouble with her.

As she reached the gap between the buildings that Scrapper had disappeared into O'Hara gave a shout behind her, and Sadie looked up to see Scrapper emerging from another building up ahead. She stopped running and turned so abruptly that she felt her ankle scream as it twisted, and found herself limping along just behind O'Hara, her gait now jerky as she ran.

"Stop where you are and put your hands in the air!" O'Hara yelled, but Scrapper didn't pay attention. Sadie saw him run into a large warehouse, the final one before the quay. The man knew the wharf better than they did, and Sadie knew their chances of catching him at this point were slim He could no doubt play this game of cat and mouse with them all day long.

She hoped he wasn't just wasting their time, running because they were FBI and represented a general threat to someone who lived on the edges of society as he did, as opposed to him actually knowing anything useful. At the moment, though, he was their only lead.

Once again, she wondered where Detective Linden was, and if he was finding out something useful while she and O'Hara ran around like jackasses over a warehouse spelunker who was unlikely to tell them anything.

Unless he was their killer. As much as she thought it unlikely, she knew better than to ever rule anyone out until they had a cast-iron alibi. And maybe not even then.

As they ran toward the warehouse there was no sign of Scrapper emerging. As the quay narrowed into the pier, even if there was a back door for him to escape from, he could only run back down the other side now, doing his best to keep out of sight as he ran between buildings.

She slowed as she got near the entrance to the warehouse.

"Go around the back," she murmured to O'Hara, "let's see if we can cut him off."

O'Hara nodded and jogged down the side of the warehouse as Sadie moved inside yet another cold, deserted building, looking for Scrapper, trying to ignore the twinges in her ankle.

This one was full of junk, from old boxes to broken pieces of electrical goods, and she guessed it was a favorite haunt of the man they were chasing.

Not least because there were plenty of places to hide.

"Scrapper?" she called into the building, alert for any indication of movement or noise. "All we want is to ask you a few questions. There's no need to panic."

Unless you're guilty, she added to herself silently.

There was no response. She scanned the back of the building for an exit, but couldn't see anything, not even a broken window. Scrapper was still in here.

Moving at a crouch with her gun stretched in front of her, checking all around her, Sadie made her way through the warehouse, turning over boxes and scrap, half expecting to find Scrapper cowering under them.

A sudden movement near her feet made her spin round, gun pointed at the floor, only to see a huge rat with a foot-long tail run over her foot.

She hated rats. As she jumped back, fighting to regain her composure, a noise further away toward the door she had just entered through caught her attention. Scrapper ran from where he had obviously been crouching behind a large crate, straight toward the entrance.

“Freeze! FBI!” Sadie yelled again as she took off after him, wondering how the hell she could have missed his presence. The guy was clearly used to hiding.

Still, there weren’t many places left to run up here. O’Hara should be able to cut him off, she thought. Although she also suspected that, with his knowledge of the quay and all of the places to hide in the abandoned buildings, Scrapper could probably play this game with them all day long.

As she ran out of the warehouse, however, there was no sign of Scrapper. She looked all around, confused that he had managed to vanish so quickly. The guy was like lightning. Sadie was no slouch; she had consistently been the fastest at track at high school and had aced her physical training at Quantico. Yet this homeless spelunker was making her feel like a bumbling idiot.

As she looked out over the pier, she could think of only one place where he had managed to hide so quickly, and that was directly over the side of the pier, hanging on just above where the murky water lapped against the edges, freezing Arctic Ocean meeting cracked and slowly thawing ice. That would be dangerous, but Scrapper clearly had no intention of being caught. Suspects who didn’t want to be caught would often go to any lengths, she thought.

As she crept forward to the side, peering over and around the edge, ready to use her weapon if Scrapper suddenly jumped up and came for her, she heard footsteps running at her close behind.

Too close. She half turned, expecting to see O’Hara, but instead Scrapper barreled into her, catching her off guard before she could get a clear shot off. Her boots caught on a patch of clear ice—the most treacherous—underfoot, and Sadie knew in a flash of horror that she was going to hit the icy water. She seemed to fall in slow motion, her whole body tensing against the inevitable cold.

Sadie wasn’t scared of water; she was as strong a swimmer as she was a runner. But there was something about bodies of icy water that had haunted her ever since Jessica’s death. The image of her sister’s body, trapped underneath a frozen lake, being pulled blue and bloated from its tomb, had stalked her dreams ever since. The image flashed in front of her eyes as the water hit her, an icy slap against the bare skin of her face above her scarf.

Almost without being aware that she was doing it, she flung an arm out, her hand closing around Scrapper’s ankle, and pulled. He crashed into the water next to her, cursing loudly, his voice high-pitched and panicked in a way that Sadie knew could mean only one thing.

He couldn't swim.

As he thrashed about, sinking under the water and coming back up again coughing and spluttering, he grabbed hold of Sadie in desperation, still kicking and pulling her down with him. Strong swimmer or not, Sadie couldn't swim against the weight of four layers of clothing, heavy boots, and another grown adult. She sank under the water, feeling the all over body shock of the intense cold.

She tried to push Scrapper off her, but he was pulling at her parka and dragging her under. An image of Jessica came to her again, struggling, her thrashing limbs losing all feeling in the freezing water.

Gathering her strength, she kicked up and her head broke above the water. She grabbed Scrapper's shoulders, hauling him up to face her as she trod water.

"Stop struggling!" she yelled at him as his panicked eyes met hers. His lips were curled back from his teeth in sheer terror, and she realized he was past the point of reason. He flailed around, threatening to pull her under again. If she couldn't get him off her, he would drown them both. She was too far from the pier to reach it and couldn't get there with Scrapper pulling her down in the other direction.

"Sadie! Grab my hand."

It was O'Hara, leaning over the side of the pier and holding a hand out to her like a lifeline.

Sadie grabbed for it but missed, feeling the icy waters close over her head.

CHAPTER SIX

Sadie felt as though she would never be warm again. Bundled up in fresh clothes that were slightly too big that had been taken from the Lost Property Office at Anchorage's main police station, and draped in blankets with a mug of scorching coffee in her hand, she felt the cold in her very bones.

Scrapper sat opposite her in the interrogation room, in his own lost and now found clothes and scratchy blankets, looking a lot cleaner than he had before he took his plunge. He was younger than Sadie would have originally guessed, maybe late thirties rather than the over fifty she would have expected from her first sightings of him. He looked at the floor, hostility and fear both radiating from him. So far, he had refused to speak to anyone, without even a thank-you for the clothes and coffee.

Detective Linden sat next to Sadie, spreading the crime scene photos out across the table with what seemed to Sadie like unnecessary relish.

He had seemed more amused than was appropriate when he had arrived on the scene at the wharf. O'Hara had managed to drag Sadie out, even with Scrapper clinging on for dear life, and then radioed Linden for help while Sadie had cuffed a now defeated Scrapper. Linden had arrived, parking his truck down at the bottom of the quay, his mouth twitching as he had taken in Sadie's drowned rat appearance.

She was really having to try hard not to hate him.

"So, what do you know about the body?" Linden barked at Scrapper. Scrapper raised his eyes and glared at the older detective.

"I don't know nothin'," he said defensively. His eyes cut to Sadie's, and she saw a hint of pleading in them. She could almost believe him, but she remembered the woman who had tipped her off about him and the way she had described Scrapper as mean enough to kill someone. The woman had been scared of him.

But just because he could kill didn't mean he had, at least not on this occasion. She wondered what his story was, and how he had ended up the way he had, homeless and foraging for anything that he could use or sell along the old quay. She had to concede that sort of life would make you mean, if only as a tactic for survival.

Linden banged his hand palm down on the table, making both her and the homeless man jump in their seats. “Don’t give me that, boy!” he roared, leaning over the table in a way that caused Scrapper to shrink back in his seat, his eyes pleading with Sadie again. Sadie fought not to react, although she didn’t approve of Linden’s tactics. He was an old-school cop, that much was clear, and although Sadie had fought to keep her temper in the interrogation room before, yelling at Scrapper like this before they had barely started to question him didn’t bode well.

She hoped they would be able to wrap this case up as fast as possible, if only so that she didn’t have to continue to work side by side with Detective Linden.

“We have it on good authority that you were at this crime scene earlier this morning,” Linden said, sitting back in his seat again and folding his arms. “So cut the crap and tell us what you saw. Because right now, boy, you’re our main suspect.”

Scrapper looked terrified. “You’re not pinning this on me!” he protested, putting his mug down on the table with shaking hands.

“The thing is, Scrapper,” Sadie cut in with a more soothing tone, trying to defuse the situation while at the same time keeping some pressure on the man, “we only wanted to ask you some questions about what you saw in there, and you ran. You resisted arrest pretty strongly. You must know how that looks?”

“Yeah,” Linden cut in with a growl, “it makes you look guilty as hell.”

Scrapper slumped in his chair, shaking his head. “Didn’t do nothin’,” he murmured, almost sulkily.

“So why did you run?” Linden demanded. “Innocent men don’t run.”

“They said they were FBI,” Scrapper said, as though that explained everything. “It’s hard enough dealing with your lot, harassing us and trying to lock us up for every little thing. Just minding our business and you treat us like scum until you think we can be useful for information. Do you know how many of us woulda died out there this winter?” He was becoming braver now, raising his voice as he went on. “Don’t see any of ya caring about that. But string some poor bitch up in the rafters and you get the Feds in before she’s even cold.”

There was silence in the small room. Linden seemed momentarily taken aback now that Scrapper had found his voice.

"So you did see the body," Sadie said coolly. She watched the realization that he had incriminated himself dawn on Scrapper's face and his expression twisted into a scowl.

"Who was it who told you, old Aggie?" he asked. "She's always been a snitch."

Linden leaned over the desk again. "I'm the one asking the questions," he snapped, ignoring Sadie as she glanced at him with her eyebrows raised.

Don't you mean "we"? she thought as Linden continued. "Now if you don't start talking, boy, I'm going to haul your ass down to the cells until you do."

Scrapper shook his head and gave a sudden grin. "Is that supposed to be a threat? As long as they're warmer than that wharf, then that sounds good to me."

Linden looked suddenly purple with rage, the veins popping out of the side of his neck. Sadie got the impression that he was fighting with himself not to haul Scrapper over the table and pummel him. Detective Linden was an angry guy, that much was obvious.

"Scrapper, a woman has been killed," Sadie said in the same cool tone she had used before, her voice cutting through the simmering tension between the two men. "If you had nothing to do with that, then we need to know what you saw. The warehouses are your haunt, aren't they? You know them like the back of your hand."

Scrapper looked proud at that comment. "Yeah, s'pose I do," he said. "I know all the hiding places anyway." He grinned again, referring to the chase he had led her and O'Hara on. Sadie smiled lightly, acknowledging his joke. She didn't like playing good cop, bad cop unless it was strictly necessary, but working alongside Linden meant it was happening naturally. She wondered if his angry style was a deliberate attempt to do just that but decided that Detective Linden was just being himself.

"So, what happened this morning, Scrapper?" she asked. Linden mercifully stayed silent, and Scrapper took a deep breath. He was going to talk.

"I saw some boys going into the warehouse and followed them," he said.

"Why did you follow them?" Linden demanded, clearly unable to stay quiet for long. "To rob them?"

Scrapper looked down, flushing red across his cheekbones. "I wanted to know what they were doing," he said defensively. "They had spray cans in their hands. Vandals."

"So you were being a good citizen?" Linden said sarcastically. "Sure you were."

"And what did you see, Scrapper?" Sadie cut in before Linden went too far and Scrapper clammed up again. Linden glared at her for interrupting and Sadie pretended that she hadn't noticed, her eyes fixed on the man across the table from them. Linden's attitude was going to fast become a liability if he didn't cut it out.

"They started poking at something up in the rafters," Scrapper said, looking down at his hands. He seemed genuinely disturbed now. "And it fell down and… there was blood everywhere. I saw her for a second…her hair." Scrapper's hands were shaking.

"And then?" Linden barked, without sympathy.

"I ran off. I knew the cops would be coming. Didn't expect FBI though." He looked up at Sadie with renewed interest in spite of his obvious upset. "Do you know who she is?"

"Do you?" Linden challenged and Scrapper clammed up again instantly. "It had nothin' to do with me," he said and went back to staring at his hands.

Sadie suppressed a sigh. Linden's tactics must work most of the time, otherwise he wouldn't be the chief detective around here, but they were off the mark with Scrapper and Sadie was getting frustrated.

He wasn't their guy.

Although a decade on the job had made her naturally suspicious, and she wasn't ruling him out entirely just yet, his story was plausible enough and as yet there was no reason to suspect him other than the fact that he had seen the boys find the body. Although killers did sometimes hang around at the scene of the crime—even, in a few infamous cases, trying to get in on the investigation—Scrapper had more reason to be hanging around the wharf than anyone else. Sadie would bet that he had seen plenty of things that had gone unreported.

"Do you have any idea who she could be, Scrapper?" Sadie asked, her voice gentle. "Has anyone gone missing that you know of?"

Scrapper shook his head. "She wasn't one of us," he told her, still looking down. Recalling the body falling and the spraying of blood had clearly distressed him, Sadie thought. "And I wouldn't know about anyone else."

"What about before you followed the boys?" Sadie went on, glad that for the moment Detective Linden was keeping quiet. "Did you see anyone hanging around the wharf who wouldn't normally be there? Anyone carrying anything wrapped in plastic, maybe?"

Scrapper shook his head. "No," he said.

"You got an alibi for last night?" Linden asked. Scrapper looked scared again, because of course, Sadie thought, he wouldn't have an alibi. None of his friends from around the campfire—or acquaintances, she recalled, remembering the woman's words—were likely to stand up in court and give him an official alibi. And they didn't yet know the time of death or how long the body had been there. Linden was just trying to scare him, which at this stage Sadie thought was unnecessary.

"I was at the tents," he said. "Aggie will tell you."

"Okay, Scrapper," Sadie said. "We will need fingerprints, DNA, and boot prints from you. Once they check out, you'll be free to go."

Scrapper looked both relieved and then disappointed, as the prospect of a night in a warm bed looked less likely.

Sadie left the room without waiting for Detective Linden, walked a little way down the corridor, and leaned back against the wall, exhaling slowly. The plunge into the sea had spooked her, and the atmosphere in the interrogation room had been oppressive. Part of her didn't want to work this case with Linden, in the heart of the Anchorage city center. She wanted to be back out in the hinterlands with Sheriff Cooper, finally finding out what had happened to Jessica.

And, if she was honest with herself, maybe more than that. She pressed the back of her hand to her lips as she remembered their kiss, a visceral memory that made them tingle. It was hard to believe it had been just a few hours before.

She blinked hard, as though doing so would snap her out of her reverie. She needed to be focused. The special agent part of her swam to the fore again as she thought about the crime scene, and about the young woman slowly bleeding out and suffocating within that coffin of plastic.

They had to catch this guy, whoever he was, before he struck again. It had been six months since the last body—unless there were others who hadn't been found.

"What was that about, Price?" Linden came out of the interrogation room, slamming the door behind him and scowling as he walked up the corridor toward her. Sadie stood up from where she was leaning against the wall, meeting his glare with a quizzical look.

"It's Agent Price," she corrected, "and I don't know what you're talking about."

"You tried to speak over me in there," he said. "This is my case and my station. You're just here to give your expertise, which I haven't seen much of yet."

Sadie swallowed her rage, knowing that biting back would only gratify him. "I'm here to work with you on this case," she said. "And you were pushing Scrapper too hard. It wasn't needed."

"I would have gotten more out of him if you had let me continue," Linden insisted. Sadie shook her head.

"He's not our guy," she said. "There was nothing more to get."

Linden made a scoffing sound. "Ruled him out already? You must be good."

Sadie was saved from finding an appropriate retort by the arrival of Agent O'Hara, coming toward them from the opposite end of the corridor. "We have a positive ID on the victim," he said, and Sadie snapped to attention, her feud with Linden—and any lingering thoughts of Sheriff Logan Cooper—forgotten.

"She's a local college girl. Victoria—Vicky—Sable. Nineteen. It was the cut to the abdomen that killed her, but toxicology is running a screen now. Her family is out of town, but they are being informed."

"Who identified the body?"

"Her roommates at college. They reported her missing yesterday morning."

Sadie glanced at Linden, who nodded. They could argue later.

"Let's go," Sadie said.

They needed to talk to Vicky's roommates. Apart from the killer, they might be the last people to have seen her alive. And that meant they might have seen the killer, too. Sadie could feel her adrenaline surge and her natural sense of justice bubbling up inside her in outrage. A killer was out there, targeting girls on the precipice of adulthood. Cutting their lives short before they had even had the chance to live them.

As Sadie left the police station with Linden and O'Hara her mind was on only one thing.

Whoever this guy was, she had to catch him before he killed again.

CHAPTER SEVEN

As they drove to Anchorage City College, Sadie read through the files that detective Linden had reluctantly given her on the first victim who had been killed six months before Victoria Sable.

Roxanne Miles. Known to her friends as Roxie.

The name immediately made Sadie think of someone confident and popular, with windswept hair and white teeth. Someone alive.

Not wrapped up in plastic and left to die.

The photographs in the file confirmed that Roxie did indeed look like Sadie had imagined her. She smiled at the camera with her head back, almost laughing, her youth and exuberance apparent. Was that what had attracted the killer to her? Sadie wondered. That combination of youth and zest for life that was the very opposite of everything this killer must stand for? That sheer aliveness. What had made him want to snuff it out?

The fact that both victims came from the college meant there was a link, that the choosing of victims wasn't purely random, a case of simply being in the wrong place at the wrong time. Either the killer had a particular grudge against female students, or he already knew both of the students. A shared teacher, maybe, or boyfriend?

Sadie hoped that questioning Vicky's roommates would give them some kind of lead, because there was very little in the file on Roxie. In fairness to Detective Linden, she could see why the case had remained unsolved.

Roxie had spent most of her time when not in class with her boyfriend, or visiting her terminally ill mother, who had since passed away. The boyfriend had a cast-iron alibi and her mother had been her only close family. She had died of cancer.

Sadie had a sudden flashback to being by her own mother's hospital bed after yet another chemotherapy session, watching her once beautiful mother shrivel away as the tumors consumed her. She hadn't been there when her mother had died. In fact, her memories of that time were hazy, but she had been less than seven years old. Even so, she remembered the news of her death being shocking but not surprising;

she had known that her mother wouldn't get better, and her illness had been going on so long it had become the norm. And then suddenly she was gone.

And no one had ever really spoken of her again, certainly not their father. Jessica and Sadie hadn't been allowed to go the funeral, and even though all of their neighbors gave them sympathetic looks and asked how they were doing in hushed voices, their mother's name was rarely mentioned. It was almost as though she had never been.

Thinking about it now, that struck Sadie as odd, because up until she had gotten ill when Sadie was four—she had only a few precious memories of her mother being well—Dawn Price had been well-known in the community. She worked as a midwife up at the hospital, and at home births when the weather prevented those living in the hinterlands from getting anywhere near the hospital.

Sadie wished she had more memories of her, but at least, she thought morbidly as she stared at the photograph of Roxie Miles, she had managed to outlive her. Mrs. Miles, already widowed, had died just after her daughter's horrific murder, having never been given the justice she deserved of knowing what had happened to her daughter. Sadie felt herself grit her teeth in anger at whoever had taken these lives so casually.

"I can see why the case was never closed," she said to Linden, who drove silently next to her and O'Hara, his eyes fixed ahead on the road but his jaw tense, resentment exuding from him.

"Can you?" he said, as though he couldn't give a damn what Sadie thought.

"There is so little to go on," Sadie continued, refusing to rise to his tone. He was working with her on this whether he liked it or not. "The boyfriend has an alibi, the girls she was friends with had already returned home for the summer break, and there were no records of anyone having a grudge against her. She simply went off campus and never came back."

Linden didn't answer. Sadie continued scanning the file and then stopped as she read more. Roxie had recently had an argument with her boyfriend about her spending a lot of time on her phone, although they had since made up. It was obvious Linden had initially suspected the boyfriend as he had checked him out thoroughly, but his alibi had held. Roxie's phone had never been found; presumably, she had taken it with her on the fateful day that she had been abducted and murdered. Linden had her laptop checked, but there was nothing unusual on it; it was clearly used purely for her studies.

If there were any leads as to who had killed her, they would be on that phone, Sadie thought in frustration. No wonder Linden was pissed about this case. As far as Sadie could see from the file, the detective had done everything that she or any other FBI agent would have done. There were just no leads. Like Vicky, there had been no fingerprints or DNA left at the scene of the crime. That would have been too easy.

Sadie looked sideways at Linden, who was still glaring at the road ahead. "It wasn't your fault," she said softly.

"What?" he snapped, although the pulse working in his jaw showed that he knew exactly what she meant.

"Roxie's murder never being solved. I would have been lost too."

Linden made a scoffing noise in the back of his throat. "That's high praise indeed," he said sarcastically, "from our local FBI hotshot herself."

Gritting her teeth, Sadie looked away. She didn't want Linden to see her rattled, because she suspected that was exactly what he wanted, but it was getting more and more difficult not to tell him where he could stick his police badge. She had been trying to be nice, damn it.

"We need to work as a team," she said drily. *Or more girls will die,* she added silently to herself.

Linden pretended not to hear her.

O'Hara was staring at the file, also trying to pretend he hadn't heard anything. There was an increasingly awkward silence as they traveled the rest of the way to the college.

*

Inside the main college building, the plump middle-aged woman at the reception desk for student accommodations took them up to the dorm that Vicky had shared with her two roommates, Cassie and Amanda. They were both white, middle-class girls from Juneau, who as the trio entered their room, were sitting together on the end of one of the beds, looking dazed. The darker-haired one had clearly been crying hard.

The other girl, who had cropped caramel hair and a stud through her nose, smiled sadly as she stood up and introduced herself as Amanda, her voice breaking on a sob.

"We just don't know who would have done this," she wailed, sitting back down. Cassie just stared at the floor, her eyes and nose red and swollen.

"I'm Special Agent Price from the FBI," Sadie said kindly, "and this is Agent O'Hara and Detective Linden from the local station. We need to ask you a few questions. I know you have already spoken to campus security and local officers, but we just need to go over a few things."

Both girls nodded. Sadie glanced at Linden, who gave her a gruff nod to indicate she should continue. Surprised that he wasn't fighting her to take the lead, Sadie continued.

"So, the last time either of you saw Vicky was the night before last?"

Amanda nodded. "Yes. She said she would be back before lights out, that she had some shopping to do. When she wasn't back by the morning, we phoned campus security."

Sadie frowned as something occurred to her. This was a college campus, full of young adults. Surely it wasn't uncommon that they sometimes stayed out all night.

"What made you automatically assume that she was in danger? Was this behavior unusual for her?"

A look passed between the two girls and Sadie knew instantly that they knew something more than they were so far telling anyone.

"Yes. She wasn't a party girl, and she doesn't have a boyfriend," Amanda quickly replied, looking away on the final word. Sadie sighed, deciding to go straight for the jugular. They didn't have time for anything else. She wanted this monster off the streets.

"Alright. What is it you aren't telling me?"

Both girls looked surprised, Amanda sitting back on the bed, her body language showing her retreating back into herself as she clammed up. Sadie was about to internally kick herself for pushing too fast, when Cassie spoke, her voice thick from her recent bout of crying.

"She had been spending a lot of time online, chatting with people. When we asked her, she just always said it was friends from back home, but she was like that, really secretive. We didn't even know that she had money problems until she said she was dropping out."

"She was dropping out?" Sadie asked, glancing at O'Hara. That could be important. She made a mental note to speak to the person who oversaw student services after they had spoken to the girls.

Amanda took over again. "Yeah, she only told us two days ago, but it turns out she has been struggling all year. She had rearranged new payment plans for her tuition fees, but she still wasn't keeping up with it. Her dad got laid off last year so her parents couldn't help. I don't know why she didn't ask me or Cassie." Amanda shook her head as she looked tearful.

"Yes, I would have helped her," Cassie said and then broke into fresh sobs. Linden sighed, looking impatient, and Sadie spoke quickly before he could say something rude.

"Why didn't you mention this when you were questioned earlier when you identified her?" she asked.

"I didn't even think about it," Amanda said, chewing at her lip. "Seeing her like that, it was awful. It was only when we were back here and we were talking about it that we thought…" She trailed off, looking uncomfortable.

"Go on," Sadie prompted, swallowing her own impatience.

"We thought maybe she had started escorting or something, to get the money, and that's why she had been so secretive online. Some girls on campus do that or webcamming to get money. But it's dangerous, isn't it, especially if she went to meet someone."

"Yes," Sadie nodded, "it's very dangerous. But so is meeting anybody you don't know from the internet. Assuming that's what has happened. Does she have a laptop?"

"It's there," Amanda said, pointing to a small desk in the corner. "We were just about to have a look at it when you came. I feel bad saying this, Vicky was a good girl, quiet. But someone did that to her…" She was silent again, a look of horror passing over her face.

Sadie walked over to the laptop, O'Hara following her. Linden was looking around the dorm room, his eyes sweeping over everything.

As she opened the laptop, she was expecting it be fruitless; most people had a password on their files, and so they would have to wait for the forensics team to get into it. But to her surprise the home screen came up unhindered. Vicky obviously trusted her roommates not to pry. Or perhaps some intuition deep within her had prompted her to leave it unprotected, just in case? Sadie shuddered as she started to open up browsers.

There was nothing to indicate that Vicky had been engaging in any type of sex work, or any dating apps. Her Messenger account, however, was a different story.

“Here,” she said to O’Hara. Linden heard her and came straight over, watching over her shoulder. “It looks as though she was arranging to meet this guy, a Brett Townsend.”

“Bit of a pretty boy,” Linden remarked. Sadie clicked on Brett’s profile picture, which showed him with his top off, staring moodily into the distance. Handsome, dark haired, with a nice body, she could see why Vicky would be flattered by the attention. According to the messages, Brett had contacted her first.

Hey beautiful, where do I know you from? You look familiar. But I’m sure I wouldn’t forget a girl as pretty as you. Pure cheese. But perhaps a quiet girl like Vicky had been flattered.

“That photo is too perfect,” O’Hara pointed out. “I know they all use filters these days, but even so.”

“Filters?” Detective Linden sounded confused. While O’Hara explained, Sadie clicked on Brett’s Facebook profile. He had no mutual friends with Vicky, and there was no mention of the college. In fact, there was no location at all.

“Do either of you know anyone called Brett Townsend? Or recognize this guy?” Sadie motioned for the two girls to come over. They both shook their heads, looking genuinely puzzled as they saw him.

“He looks like a model,” Cassie said, doubt in her voice.

Sadie nodded, her jaw tightening. “My thoughts exactly,” she said as she clicked on the rest of his pictures.

There were only a handful of them, all showing Brett in various poses. No shots of him drinking with friends, or at home with family. She went back to his profile and scrolled through his feed. There were the standard positive thinking memes, some generic posts about what a great day he was having, and music videos shared from YouTube. It looked normal enough at first glance, but there was nothing to indicate where he lived or what he did.

“That’s because he is a model,” Sadie said. “That’s a stock photo. Brett Townsend doesn’t exist.”

There was a shocked silence from the girls. Cassie’s hand flew to her mouth and Amanda took her by the arm and led her back to the bed.

“Why didn’t she tell us that she was meeting someone?” Cassie cried. She was visibly shaking.

“Because she knew we would have tried to talk her out of it,” Amanda said quietly. She shook her head. “We should have looked at her laptop when she didn't come back that night. We could have stopped it." Her eyes were haunted.

"This wasn't your fault," Sadie said, her voice quiet but firm. "There was no way that you could have known. The only person at fault is the one who did this to her." It was true, but she knew that both Cassie and Amanda would carry the guilt with them anyway, most likely for the rest of their lives.

Just as Sadie still blamed herself, all these years later, for not having saved her sister, even though there was nothing that she could have done. Just like Vicky, Jessica had simply never come home.

O'Hara had taken over with the laptop, scrolling through the last of the messages between Vicky and the mysterious Brett. "They were arranging to meet," he said excitedly, leaning closer to the screen. Sadie felt her heart beating quicker.

"When and where?" Linden barked.

"The night before last," O'Hara said grimly. "Outside the main city bus station."

Sadie looked at Linden. He had the same immediate thought as her. "Security camera footage," he said.

Sadie nodded, the adrenaline flooding her so fast she felt momentarily dizzy. They had a trail.

"Then let's get to the bus station," she said. "Right now."

CHAPTER EIGHT

Sadie followed Detective Linden into the bus station, already sensing that he intended to take the lead on this part of the investigation and having already decided to let him. Linden knew the city center better than she did, and he had been what she expected was uncharacteristically quiet when they had questioned Vicky's roommates.

This time there were just the two of them. As they had passed the police station on the way, O'Hara had gotten out of the police truck to take the laptop in to be looked at by forensics and to go over Roxie's file again, comparing it to what they now knew of Vicky.

Sadie wanted more time to study it again herself and had almost reluctantly handed it over to O'Hara, but she knew that she had to let the eager rookie agent have some responsibility. She had partnered with him on her last case, and she had thought he showed a lot of promise. Having worked with her, he was no longer quite as starstruck by Sadie as he had been either, which made working together a lot easier.

Sadie felt sure that the missing piece would be on Roxie's phone, that she had met "Brett" too, but knew that was never likely to turn up. But there was a good chance that forensics could find an IP address for "Brett."

The bus station was large and gray, the concrete floor coated with ice, and busy with buses and coaches coming and going. As Sadie followed Detective Linden toward the manager's office, she scanned the walls and ceiling as she had the outside, looking for cameras. If Vicky had met Brett here, there had to be some footage. Which meant seeing Brett's real face and identifying the killer. As much as Sadie knew that cases were rarely so easy, sometimes killers got too arrogant and slipped up. She prayed that this would be one of those times.

They reached the small office of the station manager. Sadie could see a gray shadow through the frosted office window. Linden rapped loudly, making even Sadie jump with the force of it.

"Open up, it's the police," Linden said, loudly enough that nearby commuters turned to look with interest. Sadie threw him a warning look, but Linden seemed to purposely ignore her. In fact, he was pretty much behaving as though Sadie wasn't there. It was completely different from the way he had been back at the college, and Sadie had a sinking feeling that this was just further proof of Linden's inherent misogyny; she was competent enough to question college girls, but he would handle the men.

Hoping that she was wrong, Sadie bit her tongue and resolutely faced the door, reminding herself that the reason they were here was more important than Linden's chauvinism.

The manager answered the door, looking angry at first and then shocked as he saw Linden, visibly swallowing with anxiety.

"Detective, how can I help you?" Linden must be notorious around central Anchorage, Sadie thought.

"We need to speak to you. We're investigating a murder," Linden barked. The man's eyes flew wide open, and he looked around the bus station frantically. He held the door open for them, ushering them in quickly and shutting the door behind them.

"Detective Linden," he said, sounding angry now that they were out of earshot of any eavesdropping commuters, "I don't have a darn clue what you're talking about."

Sadie took a quick glance around the cramped office. It was as she would have expected, with a small desk cluttered by timetables and highway codes, and a pinboard with more of the same. The computer looked even older than the one at Cooper's County Sheriff's station, and she smiled to herself as she remembered all the times that she had teased him about it.

"What do you know about the body found at the wharf?" Linden asked, crossing his arms and looking impatient. The station manager looked angry again and Sadie stared at Linden, wondering if this was his usual approach or if he was showboating for her benefit.

Either way, his approach sucked. The manager wasn't a suspect—at least not yet—and they needed him to show them the footage. If Linden continued to antagonize him the man had every right to tell them to get lost, which meant wasting time seeking a warrant from the chief.

The last thing Sadie wanted to do was waste time. The killer had clearly murdered Vicky the same night that he had met and abducted her, and even though—as far as they knew—there were six months between Roxie's murder and Vicky's, Sadie knew that meant nothing. Once killers got their confidence up and a taste for the thrill of the act of murder, things could escalate quickly.

Although three murders were needed for this to formally classify as a serial killer, Sadie had no doubt that was exactly what they were looking at. And until they cross-referenced with unsolved murders in other states, possibly at other colleges, they couldn't be certain that there were only two.

Or, like other serial murderers, he could have begun by targeting those who were less likely to be missed. The homeless, addicts, and runaways, for example. She made a mental note to go back to the industrial wasteland and question the tent dwellers there if any of them had gone missing in the last couple of years.

"I don't know what you're talking about," the bus station manager was saying, sounding even angrier. "And if you think you can come in here and accuse me—"

"No one is accusing you, sir," Sadie cut in soothingly, "we just need to ask you a few questions." She ignored the glare that Linden threw her way, although she could almost feel his eyes burning angrily into her face.

The manager looked unimpressed. "Haven't seen you around," he said dismissively. "You're the detective's new sidekick, then?"

Sadie bristled at the assumption and at Linden's scornful snort at the suggestion. She flashed her badge. "FBI. Special Agent Price," she said coldly. The manager stared at her badge, his face going white, before sitting down at his desk. Sadie glanced at his name badge.

"Bill," she said, "we need to get a look at your security footage from night before last. A local girl went missing and was killed, and we believe that she met her attacker here. Just outside the entrance, in fact. Is that area covered by cameras?" Sadie already knew the answer was yes, and Bill nodded, giving the information away easily. She wondered what Linden's overly confrontational attitude was about and wondered if Bill had a record or history of being obstructive. If he had, then that might explain Linden's attitude, but the detective hadn't bothered to fill her in on the information on the way there.

"We need to look at that footage immediately." Linden came back into the conversation, anger lacing his voice. "It could be crucial to my investigation."

My investigation, Sadie noted with a surge of annoyance. He was trying to establish superiority, she knew, and could have felt more sympathy toward him if he wasn't publicly dismissing her and her expertise, which would technically always outrank his. Even Deputy Sheriff Jane Cooper, Logan Cooper's sister, who had been outrightly hostile to Sadie on her arrival, had never been this obviously rude in the middle of an investigation.

She was good friends with Jane now. Sadie doubted that was ever going to happen with Detective Linden.

The manager had rallied from his initial shock at Sadie's rank, and now raised his eyebrows at them both, suddenly realizing that, for the moment, he had the upper hand.

"Don't you need a warrant for that?"

"Only if you refuse," Linden said. "But obstructing the investigation is a crime. Why would you want to unless you have something to hide? Perhaps I should take you in for questioning? Do you know Victoria Sable?"

Bill blinked in confusion at Linden's rapid-fire questions. It was a tactic that Sadie had used herself on suspects…but not someone they needed to get information from, not right off the bat. She didn't get the impression that Bill had anything to hide and was certain that if Linden had begun their exchange more politely then they would be looking at the footage by now.

"I don't know who the hell that is," Bill protested.

"Where were you two nights ago?" Detective Linden was relentless.

"I was here until midnight," Bill said defiantly. "And then I was at home with my wife. You can ask her."

Linden looked unimpressed by that. Spousal alibis, of course, were notoriously unreliable. He opened his mouth to fire off another question, but Sadie had had enough. So, she suspected, had Bill.

"Thank you for the information," she said politely, stepping forward so that she placed herself half in front of Detective Linden. He would hate her for the slight, but she was past caring. He was going to waste their time throwing his weight around trying to show who was in charge, when there were more important things to worry about.

Like just who had killed Vicky and Roxie.

"We have to question everyone," Sadie reassured Bill. "It's part of our inquiries. Now we really do need to see that footage. Someone is preying on young college girls, and we need to stop him as soon as possible."

Bill looked at her, and Sadie saw the realization slowly dawn on his face about just what his footage might show. He nodded slowly, the anger draining from his expression.

"What timeframe do you need?" he asked, turning toward his computer. Sadie had to resist throwing Linden a triumphant look. The detective looked annoyed that Sadie had succeeded in getting the information so swiftly.

"Go for between ten p.m. and midnight to start," Linden snapped. Bill brought up the footage on the screen, fast forwarding through a trickle of people coming and going from the bus station late at night. It went on and on, and Sadie hoped that Bill was going to be happy to hand over hours of footage without a warrant or they would be here all day.

Suddenly a young woman came into focus, standing outside the main hub of the station, looking around her. Waiting for someone.

"There, stop the video!" The camera paused, and Sadie and Linden leaned forward.

It was her. Vicky Sable, her blonde hair flowing over her shoulders from under her beanie hat.

"Okay," Sadie said breathlessly. "Play at normal speed."

They watched as Vicky continued waiting, looking around her more and more uncertainly. Then a man came into the camera view, walking toward her. He was bundled up in black clothes and black sunglasses, Sadie saw with a sinking stomach, and with the dim light of the station and the security cameras, it wasn't going to easy to identify him.

Linden could rule out Bill though, Sadie thought. The manager was a bit shorter and significantly fatter than the guy on the screen. He had dark hair, the ends showing under his hat. Longer and darker than the pictures of Brett.

Indeed, Vicky seemed to take no notice of him at first, until he stopped in front of her and spoke to her. His back was to the camera, but Vicky's face was in view and in spite of the grainy footage, Sadie could see the look of confusion on her face. "Brett" didn't look as she had expected. Even so, after a few moments of talking, she walked off with him. They were heading in the direction of the parking lot.

Don't get into his car! Sadie screamed silently at the girl, as though she could somehow prevent the inevitable outcome. The fact that they were watching some of Vicky's last moments alive filled her with both sorrow and rage.

"Is there footage from the parking lot?" Linden asked, staring at the screen intently. He had forgotten his hostility now, as focused as Sadie was on the screen unfolding before them.

Sadie nodded, looking at Bill with hope. They might struggle to identify the killer, but if they could see his vehicle—or whatever vehicle he was using—that gave them another piece of solid data to work on.

As transfixed as they were, Bill quickly found the parking lot footage that corresponded with the time Vicky and the man had met outside the station. Sadie was holding her breath as the image of the dark, almost empty parking lot came onto the screen.

Vicky and the man who would soon murder her came into the shot, walking across the lot. Bill panned the footage across, and they saw a single car parked in the corner. "Is that a Jaguar?" Sadie asked, recognizing the distinct shape.

"Yeah, a sports coupe, late model," Linden said. They watched as Vicky got into the car with the man and they drove off.

The angle of the camera meant that they couldn't make out the license plate, but the make and model of the car was still a lot to go on. Most people in Anchorage drove trucks and Jeeps, which were a lot more practical in an Alaskan winter than a sports coupe.

Which meant there could only be a handful of them around.

Momentarily forgetting their antagonism, Sadie and Linden gave each other a triumphant look.

They were closing in.

CHAPTER NINE

Even in the dim afternoon light, the old industrial estate was deserted. There was no one to witness their meeting.

Being back so soon, so close to where he had placed the first body, was undoubtedly dangerous, especially when crime scene investigators had only just finished crawling around, but he hadn't been able to help it. It gave him a thrill, knowing that they had nothing on him and no way to discover who he really was. "Brett" had done the job, just as he had known it would.

Of course, he knew he couldn't continue in the same vein. That profile would have to go now that it had served his purpose, dishing his prey up to him on a plate. His mouth watered at the thought of it.

At the way Vicky had struggled, and the horror on her face when his knife had entered her, cutting through her like a slab of meat. Which was all they were really. Stupid, with their eager eyes and pallid faces, walking around as if they were grown women when they truly didn't have a clue about the world or how dangerous it really was.

He was doing them a favor really. There were men out there that were a lot more dangerous than him. He could almost think of it as mercy killing.

The thought made him smile, and he fingered the long blade hidden under his coat, the feel of it and the thought of what he was going to do with it giving him a thrill that went beyond mere sex to something much more primal.

It had made him feel like a god when the life had started to drain out of Vicky's eyes. Accompanied by the inevitable terror as he had reached her head and face, wrapping her up tight.

He hadn't expected her to be found so soon, though. He would have to work faster now, while the police were still distracted by this murder to expect another one so soon.

There was no way he could wait another six months again. Roxie had been his first, and they always said you never forgot your first. It had been exhilarating but had also scared him. He had lain low, until he spotted his next victim and the urge had taken over, and this time only gotten stronger. He was riding the wave now.

His phone buzzed and he looked down at it, smiling to see that "Brett" had a new direct message. He liked being Brett, adopting a new persona, watching the way he could so effortlessly reel these girls in. It was sad that Brett would have to go, but he knew that the encryption wouldn't hold forever. It might take a while, but they would crack it eventually. No, Brett would have to go the way of his prey, and he would have to adopt yet another online persona, as he had after Roxie.

It wasn't hard to construct a convincing avatar. These girls were so *stupid*, he thought, almost with pity. So ready to believe the lies on a screen, but then they spent so much of their lives on screen perhaps they couldn't tell just what was real and what was true anymore.

The part where they realized the truth had proved to be almost as delicious as the kill itself.

The message was from her, letting him know that she was just five minutes away. That she couldn't wait to meet him and was so excited to finally see him in person. The sheer naivety of her made him laugh aloud.

He stamped his feet, rubbing his gloved hands against the cold, even as the anticipation curling in the pit of his stomach kept his body warm.

Hers would be cold, soon. It fascinated him, the way life could turn so quickly to death.

Perhaps that was why he liked to draw it out a little for them. He breathed in the cool air and felt it invigorate his lungs.

He looked up as he heard heeled boots clicking on the ice and smiled as he saw her coming toward him. Unlike him, she looked exactly like her picture, even down to the cute dimple in her cheek. She didn't take much notice of him at first, just as he had expected.

She was looking for Brett.

He stepped out in her path, greeting her by name and introducing himself, enjoying the look of confusion on her face, and then the disappointment as her bubble burst. As she realized that it really had been too good to be true all along. Of course, an absolute hunk like that wouldn't be interested in a college drop-out like her. He saw the self-doubt set in, and the urge to be polite and not show him how horrified they were that he wasn't what they expected, and he smiled to himself.

Then he saw the realization dawn that she had seen him before and that he was kind of familiar and knew that he had to act fast.

He smiled, showing his teeth.
No, he wasn't Brett. Brett didn't exist.
And very soon, neither would she.

CHAPTER TEN

Sadie tapped her fingers impatiently on the desk as she sat next to Linden, waiting for his computer screen to load the results of their search for local owners of the make of Jaguar that Linden had identified. The killer may well be from out of town, or even using a stolen car, but it gave them somewhere to start from at least.

So far, they had nothing else. Not only had the killer left no DNA or fingerprints, but the profile for the mysterious Brett was proving a hard nut for the FBI cyber team to crack. A terse phone call from their cyber expert had let Sadie know that their search analyses had so far yielded nothing, not even a basic IP address.

"Brett" had safeguarded his real identity with sophisticated firewalls and encryption, indicating that their killer was either an IT whiz, or was working with someone who was. They were services that could be bought, and some cyber freelancers were happy not to ask just what it was they were being asked to hide.

Cybercrime in general was becoming more and more of a problem, Sadie knew, not least because law enforcement and their teams of experts couldn't seem to keep up with all the innovative ways in which criminals could use the world wide web to perpetuate and hide both their crimes and their identities. In the case of a killer like "Brett," it made it easier for him to target his victims and to leave no trace.

She could only hope that for all his internet and crime scene evasion, he had been stupid enough to use his own car.

Next to her, Detective Linden was muttering under his breath, as impatient as she was. He hadn't said a word to her on the drive back to the station, and Sadie had bitten her own tongue, still angry about the way he had approached things with the bus station manager. If she hadn't been able to smooth things over then they would be sitting around on their asses right now waiting for a warrant.

The animosity coming from Linden was palpable, however, and Sadie wondered if she should tackle the subject now before the atmosphere between them soured even further. They had to work together on this whether either of them liked it or not, and Vicky and

Roxie deserved more than to have justice delayed because the lead detective on their case couldn't get his head out of his ass.

She took a deep breath, ready to broach the subject, when Linden surprised her by bringing it up first. "You undermined me in there. Don't do that again. You could hold things up."

Sadie looked at him with a mixture of outrage and confusion. "You think I could have been the one to hold things up?" she retorted. "You were way too heavy-handed in there. It was uncalled for. If I hadn't stepped in, he was about to refuse to let us see the footage."

Linden swiveled in his chair, glowering at her. "You're telling me how to conduct a murder investigation?" He said it as though Sadie was fresh out of kindergarten. "Listen, girl, I have been doing this a lot longer than you have."

"You can call me Special Agent Price," Sadie snapped, resisting the urge to punch him straight in the nose and show him how much of a girl she was. "And just how many serial killers have you brought down, Detective Linden?"

He looked taken aback for a moment, as though he had expected her to wilt in the face of his anger. "I was dealing with murderers before you were even in diapers," he rejoined, adding, "We don't have enough bodies to label this a serial yet."

"And I'm hoping we never do," Sadie snapped back. "If you go around upsetting everyone that we need information from, we will waste time."

"And if you don't back off and let me do my job," Linden came back at her, fast as a whip, "we will waste even more."

They were at a stalemate, glaring furiously at each other. Sadie took a deep breath, saying through gritted teeth, "Look. We have to work together whether we like it or not. And I'm suggesting you be less heavy-handed until it's actually necessary."

She could see how Linden could be fantastic in the interrogation room with a tough suspect. The type that understood little but brute strength and saw negotiating as weakness. But if he went around applying that attitude to every situation, it could only be obstructive.

"Okay." Linden shrugged, surprising her.

"Okay?" Sadie repeated, caught off guard by what seemed like a sudden change of heart.

"You did a good job with those girls," he said, referring to Victoria Sable's roommates. "I could see that, so I stayed out of it. Women are good with women, I appreciate that. But when it comes to the local guys, you let me handle it. You're too soft."

Sadie felt her eyebrows fly up her forehead and for a moment she was lost for words at Linden's unashamed sexism.

"If I was 'soft,' Detective, I wouldn't have brought the Boston Mangler in," she said quietly, referring to the case last year that had made her an American hero in the eyes of the public.

It was a case that still kept her up at night and that she was still waiting to hear the outcome of an investigation on, but Linden didn't need to know that.

Linden was momentarily lost for words at that, and Sadie was steeling himself for his next dismissive remark when the computer screen beeped, taking their attention off one another and back to the task at hand.

Sadie stared at the screen. This was too good to be true, she thought.

"There's only one hit?"

Detective Linden clicked on it; his eyes lit up with an anticipation that Sadie recognized. He was as invested in this case as he was, she reminded herself. They had to find a way to work together. Even if he was a chauvinistic jerk.

Linden shook at his head. "I should have known," he said as he read the information on the screen. Sadie peered at it and then frowned.

"Kent Westwood? Why does that name seem familiar?"

"Don't you read the papers?" the older detective asked.

Sadie shook her head. "Not unless I have to." Even so, she knew that she had heard the name being bandied about, probably in Caz's saloon amongst the regulars at the bar, who were notorious for gossip after a hard day.

"Likes to think of himself as a man-about-town," Linden said scornfully. He reached for a newspaper at the back of his desk and tossed it to her. "Headline on page five," he directed her.

Sadie read the story, which was a double-page spread, featuring the profile of a man who, Sadie noticed right away, could easily be an older version of the so-called Brett. She felt a fizzing in her stomach, her intuition prodding at her. Something about this guy unsettled her just from looking at his picture, although she admitted to herself that it could be no more than an immediate distrust of anyone who cultivated the slick playboy image that Kent Westwood was clearly going for.

He was a property developer, originally from California, with the baked-in tan and shiny white veneers to show it. Probably Botox too, she thought, unless tabloid photographers had taken to applying Instagram-style filters to their pictures. The paper described him as early forties, but his forehead and eyes were noticeably absent of wrinkles. Not that there was anything wrong with that, Sadie acknowledged, but it all came together to give him the appearance of a very rich, very successful man-about-town as Linden had referred to him.

The newspaper story was about the real estate that Westwood was building and renovating in central Anchorage, often taking run-down areas and gentrifying them. The story was largely positive, praising him for the uptick in people moving to Anchorage and tourists coming to stay in his five-star holiday homes and Airbnbs. Only a paragraph was devoted to the opposite view of a social worker complaining about the effects of gentrification on the original locals to the area, working-class people, people of color, and single mothers whom Westwood needed out of the way.

"A lot of difference between him and our first suspect," Sadie murmured, thinking of the glaring disparity between this man and Scrapper. She wondered how many people could potentially end up homeless thanks to Westwood and his gentrification plans.

"Any history?" Sadie asked.

To his credit, Detective Linden was already running the search. "Nothing. He's clean."

"Think he's our guy?"

Linden looked doubtful. "Look at him. He doesn't need to put fake profiles on the internet to lure women, does he? Only to use his own car. But we've got to start somewhere."

Pleasantly surprised by the "we," Sadie stood up, nodding.

"Let's go and talk to him."

As she followed Linden out of his office, she wondered what they were about to find. Linden was right; Westwood didn't need fake model pictures to lure women, even college girls twenty years younger than himself. Sure, it could be an attempt to cover his tracks, and the car a stupid mistake, but the profile the newspaper gave of the man, and the mind behind the killings, didn't seem to fit somehow, no matter how much she tried to tell herself that it was far too early to make that judgment call.

But Sadie had been trained in the Behavioral Analysis Unit, and probably knew more about the inner workings of the average serial killer than she did her best friends. These killings, whatever they were about, didn't strike her as being about sex, regardless of the Brett profile and the flirtatious messaging. There had been no indication on either Roxie's or Vicky's body to suggest a sexual motive.

Perhaps she was guilty herself of making snap judgments of Westwood, given his playboy persona. Perhaps he had a hidden hatred of women that he hid underneath his public face. As Sadie took a last glance at the newspaper before she shut the office door, she couldn't help thinking that for all his obvious good looks, Westwood's dark eyes were sharklike. Predatory.

Sadie would bet her last dollar that Kent Westwood had some dark secrets.

And she intended to go and find out just exactly what they were.

CHAPTER ELEVEN

The sun was setting by the time Sadie and Linden reached Kent Westwood's downtown mansion, the six hours of daylight already coming to an end.

Sadie had been back in Alaska for over two months and had arrived in the dead of winter, so she had readjusted to the dark and the cold, but this evening she felt suddenly chilled. As she watched the sun spreading orange across the sky, she realized how much she missed the Southern climate.

Westwood's home was certainly something she would have expected to see by the beach in California, rather than in the suburbs of Anchorage. Looking at the large, frosted windows and balconies, it was clear that Westwood wasn't trying to blend in.

Could he really be their guy? It was tempting to think that he couldn't fit the profile, but Sadie had worked enough cases to know that, while most people were predictable, even serial killers, they could also never fail to surprise. If Westwood was the killer, then in many ways he was hiding in plain sight.

Perhaps he thought he was untouchable and using his own car to pick up his victims so brazenly was less a foolish mistake and more an indication of his arrogance. Narcissism was a fairly reliable trait in psychopaths.

Linden buzzed at the front door, and Sadie wondered how this interrogation was likely to go. She didn't want a repeat of the way he had questioned—or rather, threatened—the bus manager.

A maid answered the door, smiling at them through heavily glossed lips. The smile failed to reach her eyes when Linden barked out an introduction.

"Detective Linden, Anchorage Police Department. This is Federal Agent Price. We need to talk to Kent Westwood."

The woman looked from Linden to Sadie as though she thought this may be some kind of joke, then her eyes widened as she realized they were serious.

"Er, Mr. Westwood is upstairs, relaxing," she said in a breathy voice. "If you wait in the foyer, I'll go and get him."

She ushered them inside, into a large reception area with a huge central staircase that went up to the floor above. The floor was marbled.

"Nice," Sadie remarked, glancing around. Linden snorted. "More money than taste, if you asked me," he said, and Sadie smiled.

Her smile faded as she watched the maid walking up the stairs, going slowly on her heels. She wore a traditional maid's outfit that Sadie thought was only just on the right side of appropriate, reminding her of the sort of outfit you would see at a costume party. The girl was incredibly pretty too, and young. Sadie was pretty sure that she had been employed for other reasons than her hospitality skills.

She glanced at Linden and saw that he was watching the maid too, his eyes narrowed. "He likes them young, doesn't he?" he murmured in a low tone that was almost a growl.

A few minutes later Westwood appeared, walking casually down the staircase. He was even more handsome than he had been in his picture and moved with the sort of effortless confidence that couldn't be faked. Kent Westwood had complete and utter faith in himself.

As he got closer, Sadie saw that she was right about his eyes, however. They still reminded her of a shark.

A predator.

"Detective," Westwood said warmly, although those eyes were like steel. "How can I help you? I hope there hasn't been a spate of break-ins in the area again. I wasn't impressed with the way you guys handled that last year."

"No," Linden said sharply. "That isn't why we are here. Where were you the night before last?"

Westwood looked surprised, and then angry. "I was here, with a friend. All day and all night. She will corroborate that, naturally."

"I'm sure she will," Sadie said in a low voice. Westwood looked at her for the first time, or rather, he looked her over, sweeping his gaze up and down her body and lingering on her breasts. When he met her eyes to find her glaring at him, he simply smiled in a way that was almost condescending. Like Linden, he was a misogynist, Sadie thought, but of an entirely different kind.

It was a kind that made the hairs on the back of her neck stand up. Sadie didn't scare easily. She had faced down men who were, on paper at least, a lot more terrifying than Kent Westwood. Yet there was something about this man that made her instincts scream at her to get as far away from him as possible.

She would rather be chained to someone like Linden for the rest of her life than spend an hour alone with this man, she realized.

"Why are you asking me all these questions? Should I call my lawyer?" Westwood was still smiling, and his tone was light, almost amused, but his flinty eyes were cold. He was angry that they were questioning him, Sadie thought, but was that because he was scared of getting caught or because his giant ego resented the intrusion?

"Do you know a woman named Victoria Sable?" Linden asked. Sadie watched Westwood's reaction closely, but she could read nothing from his expression.

"I know a lot of women," he said casually. "I don't think I recognize that name, though."

Sadie took out a picture of Vicky from her pocket and showed it to him. Westwood gave it a quick glance, one perfectly plucked eyebrow raised.

"Pretty," he said with appreciation. "But no, I don't know her. Why?"

"Where were you at six p.m. day before yesterday?" Linden said.

"I told you," Westwood snapped, starting to lose patience, "I was here. With an …acquaintance. Debra Wyle. I'll give you her contact details."

"You weren't at the bus station, picking up Victoria Sable in the car park?"

"I told you…" Westwood began, only to be interrupted again by Linden.

"Who is Brett?"

Linden's rapid-fire, almost aggressive questions were disorientating Westwood, who looked momentarily lost for words. He opened his mouth to say something, but then closed it again. For the first time since they had arrived, he wasn't controlling the conversation.

There were some suspects, Sadie thought, who Linden's approach was definitely appropriate for. She was happy to take a back seat on this one, taking the chance to carefully study Westwood and his reactions.

He was hiding something; Sadie was a hundred percent certain of it.

"I don't know what you're talking about, Detective. I was here, with Debra. You can check with both her and my maid." There was a slight smirk at the corner of his mouth as he said it, a hint of something that made Sadie's skin crawl. She decided that she didn't want to think about the relationship between Westwood and his "maid."

At the same time, she wondered if the girl went to the local college. Westwood's propensity to have beautiful young women around could be the obvious link, she thought. To a financially struggling college student, she imagined the prospect of working for Westwood could seem initially lucrative.

"How many other young women do you have working for you?" Linden asked, and Sadie realized that Linden was thinking along the exact same lines as she was.

"Just what are you implying, Detective?"

"Are you sure you don't recognize Victoria Sable? Maybe she worked for you too?"

Westwood's face took on a purple hue underneath his very un-Alaskan tan. "I've told you; I don't know who she is!"

"Oh," Linden said flatly. "That's quite strange, because we have video footage of a man who looks like you, in a car that looks exactly like yours, picking her up evening before last. A few hours before she was murdered."

Tan or not, Westwood now went white. He took a step back, distancing himself from them and their accusations.

"Leave," he said, his voice now as cold as his eyes. "If you want to talk to me again, you'll need a warrant. And I will have a solicitor."

He walked to the door and opened it for them. *Aren't you going to get your maid to do that?* Sadie thought, biting back the sarcastic retort at the last minute. Antagonizing him further wasn't going to help.

He slammed the door shut behind them, and Sadie walked quickly back toward the police truck, only realizing that she was holding her breath when she reached it and exhaled slowly. Westwood put her nerves on edge. Sadie had unfortunately had enough experience with predators in her career to recognize one when she saw them. His whole demeanor, along with the heavy circumstantial evidence and the creepy undercurrent that she sensed between him and his maid, pointed in only one direction that she could see.

She looked up at Linden, who had a deep scowl across his face. "He's guilty," Sadie said firmly. To her surprise, Linden nodded firmly.

"Yeah. We can agree on that. But his alibi will check out, I'm sure of it. That girl in there, and this other woman, I reckon they will lie for him."

"Let me work on that," Sadie suggested, resisting the obvious comment that Linden seemed to think only women could communicate with women.

Linden gave a curt nod as he opened the truck and got in. Sadie slid into the other side, feeling despondent. She had the sinking feeling that Linden was right. And with a solid alibi and no actual license plate for the car in the footage, they didn't have enough evidence against Westwood to get a warrant.

She needed to work on the maid, she thought. Find out just how long she had been worked for Kent Westwood, and just what she had seen behind the walls of his mansion. Even if she was in thrall to her employer, even the most dedicated accomplice could slip up under pressure.

Sadie felt drained, as though being around Westwood had sucked all of the energy out of her. It had been a long day, especially as she had been up in the early hours with Cooper, following her father's map. It felt as though it had happened a long time ago, not in the last twenty-four hours. She needed to get back to the saloon, eat, and sleep.

And, maybe, see Sheriff Cooper.

They had plenty to talk about.

As Linden started the truck, Sadie laid her head back on the seat rest, looking forward to her bed and a good night's sleep. She could come at this case better with a clear head.

Then Sadie's phone rang, just a beat before Linden's also rang, and Sadie knew instantly that her much needed sleep wasn't going to happen.

"Sadie?" It was Golightly, and his tone of voice told her all that she needed to know.

"What is it?" She held her breath, hoping that she was wrong, a shiver running down her spine at Golightly's next words.

"You need to get back down to the wharf," Golightly said. "There's another body."

CHAPTER TWELVE

Sadie strode into the warehouse feeling anger bubbling up in her, masking the horror that lurked underneath. Linden was wearing much the same expression and neither of them had spoken a word on the journey across the city to the wharf.

He did this right under our noses. While they had been questioning Westwood, even, this young woman had been dying, bleeding out into her shroud of plastic wrapping. The swiftness of it, at finding another body barely twelve hours after the first, had Sadie reeling.

As well as the Anchorage police chief, O'Hara, and the forensics team, Golightly was there too this time, hands stuffed deep into his pockets as he watched the body being carefully handled by the forensics team and the plastic being carefully cut away.

"How long has she been here?" Sadie asked, dispensing with pleasantries. One of the forensics team looked up at her. He had been here this morning too, and he looked slightly dazed, as though he couldn't quite believe the situation was repeating itself so soon either.

"The ME will be the best judge of that, but it's pretty clear that she was killed recently. The body is fresh; the wound is still bleeding."

Sadie found that this time she couldn't look at the body. Instead, she glanced across at O'Hara, who gave her a shocked look back. "This is escalating fast," he said quietly. Sadie nodded.

"Unless he held her for a while," she said. Linden looked doubtful, although at least his expression seemed genuine now, rather than the scornful dismissal he had displayed all day. She suspected Linden was grappling with the implications of this just as hard as she was.

"Why her and not Vicky? And no one's been reported missing."

"I hear you. My immediate feeling is the same; she's been taken today and killed within a few hours. But we can't make assumptions. And is it the likeliest possibility? That he has struck again so soon, and dumped the body so near to where he left Vicky's? He could so easily have been caught."

Sadie looked around the warehouse, looking everywhere but at the body, but not out of squeamishness. She had seen too many crime scenes for that, but because although she knew that logically there was nothing she could have done to prevent this, she felt responsible somehow. She was supposed to be the behavioral expert; what signs had she missed that could have indicated another abduction and murder so quickly?

She knew there was nothing, but on some level, it was easier to try to blame herself than admit that this killer was running rings around them, and they had no idea who he was.

Unless it was Westwood. He might have alibis, but she was inclined to disbelieve him and the women willing to lie for him. Until they had a better idea of the timeframe required and exactly how long the body had been here, they couldn't entirely rule him out.

The fact that they could have been questioning him just a short time after he had killed his latest victim filled Sadie with horror. No wonder he had been defensive.

"Are you all right, Price?" Golightly barked at her, and Sadie realized that she was staring across the warehouse without so much as blinking. She nodded sharply, coming back into focus.

"Just mulling things over," she said, glancing at Linden. "We were just questioning Kent Westwood—"

"The guy who's bought up half the city's prime real estate?" the police chief asked sharply. Sadie nodded, but Linden cut in, answering his superior for her.

"We have footage from the bus station of Victoria Sable getting into what we can only assume was the killer's car, with the killer. The license plate isn't visible, but the make and model is the only one in the area and matches Westwood's car. The man in the video is wrapped up with sunglasses and hat, but his build and what we can see of his coloring matches Westwood well enough."

Golightly whistled under his breath, but the chief looked annoyed.

"And you think it's him? You'll need better evidence than that before you get a warrant to haul him in, Linden. The man is very rich and very litigious, and I don't need to tell you that APD can't afford to get sued."

"He's got an alibi," Sadie said, "and I doubt he had time to do this and then get home before we turned up."

It didn't escape her notice that the Anchorage police chief looked relieved, and she couldn't help but wonder just how deep Kent Westwood's pockets went. Golightly, however, looked skeptical at her words.

“I know you, Price,” he said. “What’s the ‘but’?”

Sadie shrugged. “There isn’t one, except that if there was a prize for acting as guilty as hell, then Westwood would win it hands down. There’s something off about him. He’s a predator. And the killer having the same build and car? You know what I think of coincidences, sir.”

“And you, Detective Linden?” The chief looked less than impressed with Sadie’s summation and was obviously surprised—though perhaps not as much as Sadie herself—when the older detective jumped in to defend her.

“Agent Price is right. We need to keep some heat on Westwood. There’s something going on there. Perhaps he has an accomplice, and this is the work of two men.”

“Or a copycat?” O’Hara suggested, then blushed. “I suppose it’s a bit too quick for that.” Sensing his embarrassment, Sadie nodded at him in encouragement.

“I have thought about that possibility regarding Roxie’s murder,” she said. “Especially now. Why wait six months between victims one and two, then two days between two and three? Unless something has set him off and he’s in the middle of a spree…which means he won’t stop here, either.”

“Opportunity,” Linden said gruffly. “Maybe he’s been in prison or traveling.”

“If he’s been out of the state, maybe he never did stop,” Sadie said quietly, feeling nauseous at the possibility of an as yet undetected trail of plastic-wrapped bodies scattered across America. She looked at O’Hara. “Go through the database,” she told him, “and check for similar crimes across the entire country over the last six months.”

O’Hara nodded. “It will be easy enough to find out if that’s the case. This is a pretty unique MO.”

“Same smell of fish, too,” the forensics guy commented. “It’s faint, but it’s there. However they are being transported, they’re coming into contact with fish or something that smells like them.”

“I’ll get two more officers on the wharf tomorrow and start questioning all the local fishermen,” the police chief said. Sadie refrained from pointing out that there had been officers doing that today, and the killer had still gotten past them.

Whoever he was, he knew the wharf and the old warehouses well, a trait she wouldn’t automatically associate with Westwood. She thought of Scrapper, the homeless guy they had questioned that morning, who had managed to hide from herself and O'Hara so effectively. Was it possible they were working together?

That Westwood, perhaps, was paying Scrapper to dispose of the bodies? The only time she had been close to Scrapper before he had changed his clothes was when she had pulled him into the water with her, but she would bet that he didn't smell too good.

"He's got a type," Linden said, cutting through her thoughts. He was staring at the victim, his expression unreadable.

Sadie grimaced as she looked over toward the body, forcing herself to finally take in the scene. Like Victoria Sable, she was slight and fair with long hair, but brunette this time rather than blonde. She felt almost certain that she would turn out to be another college girl.

"If she's another student," Linden said, following her gaze and seeming to read her mind, "then I would wager the link is at that college rather than the wharf. We need to get down there first thing in the morning."

"Yeah," Sadie said, trying not to show her surprise at his sudden display of teamwork. He was clearly shocked and, if as she suspected he blamed himself for not solving Roxie's murder, this would have hit him hard. She was sure he would be back to his belligerent self once the situation had sunk in.

At the mention of morning, she realized they were now rapidly approaching bedtime. The wharf had been swathed in darkness when they had arrived. If she wanted to get home, it was a long drive out into the hinterlands; she would be better off sleeping over at the Anchorage Field Office.

Who am I kidding? she thought wryly. There was no way she would be getting any sleep after this. She couldn't see Linden clocking out either. She would be working this case until they found whoever was murdering young women and trussing them up in plastic.

Or at least until Golightly, who was aware of Sadie's innate tendency to push herself until she dropped, ordered her to go and get some sleep.

"Bunk up at the Field Office. There's not much more that can be done until we have an ID and the information from forensics," Golightly said, glowering at her in anticipation of a comeback. Sadie glanced at Linden, expecting him to argue with Golightly, but he looked relieved, and Sadie remembered that he was an older guy and it had been a long day.

"But he could be out there hunting his next victim," she protested.

"We have the college on alert," the police chief told her, "and a bulletin going out on the radio. I'll be doing a press conference tomorrow. But ASAC Golightly is right. Without any leads on this guy or an ID on this new victim, we can't do anything right now. We'll be in touch immediately if we need you."

Sadie wanted to argue that it was now the other way around. The killings might all be local, but this was now clearly a serial killer. Her jurisdiction.

But she suddenly felt too tired to argue.

Perhaps everyone was right, and sleep was just what was needed. Even so, she sighed as she walked out of the warehouse and toward the FBI snowcat with Golightly and O'Hara.

As they reached the truck, Golightly pulled Sadie to one side.

"This probably isn't the best time, Price," he said in his gruff voice, "but I've heard from Internal Investigations about the Mangler case."

Sadie felt herself go cold. Ever since relocating to Alaska, the Mangler case had followed her. Not only did the sadistic killer, who had come so close to abducting Sadie herself before she had managed to overpower and kill him, haunt her nightmares—though not as frequently as Jessica these days—but Quantico had opened an investigation.

Had Sadie really needed to kill him? Had she acted purely in self-defense? She was confident that she had done nothing wrong.

Technically, at least.

But in her darkest moments, she knew that in that split second when she had put a bullet in the Mangler's head, it hadn't been purely self-defense that had motivated her. It had been sheer, unadulterated hatred. Months of hunting one of the most sadistic serial killers ever known had taken its toll on the entire task force, which Sadie had fronted. He had deserved to die.

But who was she to make that decision? She knew that if someone in her position ever crossed those moral lines, then they were in danger of becoming just like the monsters they hunted. And although she knew her professional conduct was impeccable, she wondered if somehow, the powers-that-be at Quantico had somehow known just how close to that line the Mangler had pushed her.

"What did they say?" she asked Golightly, holding her breath, telling herself that it must be good news, or he would be relieving her of her badge.

But instead, it was no news.

"They are ready to render a decision. I asked them to give you a bit of breathing space; explained that you were in the middle of a new serial killer investigation. Stressed what a damn good agent you are. But I can't do more than that. You'll be hearing from them by next week."

Sadie let out her breath, watching it turn to a visible vapor in the freezing air, lit up by the headlights of the snowcat. It hadn't escaped her that if Golightly thought he needed to buy her some time, then he was expecting it to be bad news.

She hadn't even thought about what she would do if her career in the FBI was over.

She wasn't going to think about it now, either.

"Thanks for telling me," she said, turning away and getting into the vehicle.

She already knew that there was no way she was going to get to sleep tonight. As soon as Golightly had gone home, she would be back on the case.

Doing her job while she still had it.

CHAPTER THIRTEEN

Sadie eyed the front of Westwood's mansion, now mostly dark except for one lit up window on the fourth floor. His Jaguar was parked conspicuously in the front drive. He was home, but was he alone?

She wasn't sure why she had put herself on unofficial stakeout on Westwood, but after driving around the city for a while she had concluded that there wasn't a lot else that she could do. She had the victim's files next to her on the seat, and she had already gone over them three times, cursing each time when she discovered no new lead. No seemingly innocuous snippet of information that could unlock the whole case.

What if Westwood had another victim in there?

She was trying to concoct a valid reason to knock on his door that wouldn't be construed as police harassment when her phone rang. It was just after midnight. Expecting it to be a breakthrough from forensics, she snatched it up, then felt a dissonant mixture of both excitement and disappointment when she saw that it was Sheriff Cooper.

"Hey, Cooper," she said softly, and then yawned.

"Long day, huh?" he said with sympathy. "I popped into the saloon, and Caz told me you would be staying down in the city. How's it going?"

"Tough. There's been another victim." She filled him in on the details, glad to be able to have him to bounce ideas off. She had always worked well with Cooper, even when they were bickering. They made a good team.

She couldn't imagine ever being able to say the same thing about Detective Linden.

Cooper laughed when she told him about the older detective and his belligerent approach. "Yeah, I've worked with Linden before. He likes to be in charge, and he's pretty old-fashioned about women."

"You're telling me," she muttered, but she was already smiling. Just the sound of Cooper's laugh, which she felt as though she knew almost intimately now, made her feel warm inside. She had been fighting her feelings for Logan Cooper for some weeks, but toward the end of their last case together had finally had to admit to herself that she was falling for him.

A visceral memory of their kiss came back to her, and she felt her lips tingle. There was no way in hell that she would admit it to him, but she wanted nothing more at that moment than for him to be there with her.

And not just to bounce ideas off.

Cooper cleared his throat, hesitating, and she wondered if he was going to mention the kiss.

"I've been thinking about this morning," he said in a low voice.

"Me too," she said. "We need to talk, don't we? About where this is going." It was the first time she had admitted out loud that they were going anywhere, and she surprised herself with the words.

Then she blushed deep crimson as Cooper said, sounding amused, "I was talking about your father's map, but yeah, I'm glad you mentioned it. I thought you would try and pretend our kiss never happened, Price. I'm glad you're finally facing the fact that you are falling in love with me."

"I am *not* falling in love with you," she snapped, but then wondered if that was even true.

"Well, I'm getting close to it, Price," he said with such frank honesty that Sadie was momentarily speechless. On some level, she had known for some time that the sheriff had feelings for her that went way beyond the simple fact that she was an attractive woman, but to hear him state it so casually shocked her. Just when had they crossed that barrier?

"Cooper…I…" Sadie's words trailed off as she tried and failed to articulate the swarm of emotions that were rising in her.

"Don't worry, Price," Cooper said softly. "I don't want to scare you off. We'll talk when you get back."

"Okay," she said quietly, feeling dazed. Sadie was good at compartmentalizing—she had to be—but the day's events were catching up with her. Two murders in one day, the news from Golightly, Cooper's kiss, and the potential breakthrough on Jessica's murder…her mind felt frazzled.

"You said you called about my father's map?"

"That doesn't matter now either," Cooper said. "You sound exhausted. Let's talk about that when you get back too."

Sadie shook her head before she remembered that Cooper couldn't actually see her. "No," she protested. "I need the distraction right now before I fall asleep in my car. What is it?"

"Well," Cooper began, "you remember those pencil marks on the back of the map, that we assumed were literally just marks, but then you said they looked vaguely familiar?"

"Yes." Sadie cast her mind back to when her father had died, and the nurse had handed them the crudely drawn map. "But in the end, we decided they were nothing."

"Right," said Cooper. "But they were niggling at me. So I copied them and checked it out, and they are Inuit words."

"Inuit?" Sadie echoed, trying to make sense of the information. What did native languages have to do with Jessica? They had both had Inuit friends at school, but while Sadie had learned a little of the language thanks to her friend Mona, Jessica had never learned any, as far as she remembered. Their mother's nurse work had sometimes taken her into the Inuit village, but she had never taken either daughter with her.

"Don't you speak it? I heard you, that time when we were hunting the Ice Man."

"Some, but I don't know the letters. I can speak it a little, but not read it. But Cooper, this doesn't make any sense. My father had nothing to do with the Inuit from the village; in fact, he moaned at my mother for going there. And Jessica didn't speak Inuit. Are you sure you're not mistaken?"

"I was told it said 'Mother Dawn.'" Cooper's voice was uncharacteristically nervous.

"Dawn? That was my mother's name." Sadie felt as though her head was spinning. She was beginning to wish she had told Cooper to leave it after all. None of this was making any sense.

"I know. Listen, Sadie." Cooper cleared his throat. "I've always wondered about this, but as you've never mentioned it, I didn't think it was right for me to bring it up—"

"Cooper," she cut in, her impatience getting the better of her. "What the hell are you talking about?"

"Your mother's disappearance," Cooper said flatly. "Haven't you ever wondered if it might be connected to your sister's murder?"

The whole world—or what she could see of it at least—seemed to go out of focus and then back in again, as though reality had somehow rearranged itself.

"Cooper," she said slowly, "my mother died of cancer."

There was a long silence.

"I know she had cancer," Cooper said, "it's in her file. Terminal. But she very definitely disappeared, Sadie. I had the records in front of me earlier today, after I was told what the Inuit stood for. I mean, it could be a coincidence, of course. I don't know if 'Mother Dawn' refers to something else. But given that it was your father who wrote it…I assumed he was indeed pointing you toward your mother. I thought you might know why he would write it in Inuit."

"Cooper, slow down. What do you mean, my mother disappeared? I remember my father telling me and Jessica very clearly that she had died. From the cancer…. I mean, we knew she was dying. I remember her in the hospital. You must have made a mistake."

Sadie was shaking her head to herself in the dark, refuting what she could already hear was the truth in Cooper's words. If there was a file, then it had to be true. Her mother had been reported missing.

"So you're saying she never showed up? But there was a funeral." Which Jessica and I weren't allowed to go to, she remembered, recalling how she had hated her father for keeping them away. She remembered, too, how he never spoke about their mother to them again, and never let anyone else speak about her in their presence either. She had always thought that was just more evidence of her father's meanness, but now she had to wonder, was it to keep them from finding out the truth?

"There was a memorial service, Sadie, not a funeral. Attended by just a few people. Townsfolk who didn't know your family well might have assumed she had died from the cancer, I don't know. We're from Juneau, so this is all new to me. But the file is here. I'll show it to you."

"But if she disappeared," Sadie said, feeling as though she was speaking through molasses, struggling to form her words as she tried to think through all of the implications, "surely there was a search? Was there never a body?"

"She was never found, and as there was no indication of foul play, the consensus was that your mother had gone off to die alone, perhaps so that you two didn't have to see it. That seems to be what your father thought, too, so he was happy for the case to be closed. Honestly, the sheriff in charge back then seems to be completely incompetent."

"I don't know what to say." Sadie stared out the window. The light in Westwood's window had dimmed. Perhaps he was finally going to bed. "Do you think my father did it?" Her words came out in a rush.

"Was he violent to your mother?"

Sadie swallowed, remembering. "Not violent, so much, but…angry. He was worse after she died…disappeared. That's when his drinking got really bad." She had to wonder now if that was because of guilt.

The hand that held the phone to her ear was shaking. In fact, she realized, feeling strangely disassociated from her physical self, her whole body was shaking.

Her mother hadn't died. Or at least, not in the way Sadie had always thought that she had. But then where was the body?

"Cooper, what if the map wasn't about Jessica at all? Maybe he really doesn't know who killed her. What if the map…is about my mother?"

"That's what I was thinking," Cooper admitted. "I mean, it has her name on it."

"In a language he didn't speak."

Or maybe he did. Sadie was starting to realize that she knew very little about her parents and her past. In fact, her whole life was starting to feel like one big lie.

"Cooper, I have to go. This is too much to take in right now. I'll call you tomorrow."

"Of course." He sounded strangely formal now, the flirting of just moments ago forgotten. "I shouldn't have told you tonight. I just…I didn't know that you didn't know."

"How could you? It's not your fault, Logan." She used his first name, and it felt odd on her tongue. "As soon as I've caught whoever is kidnapping students and gutting them like fish, we need to go and check out that cave."

As she replaced her phone in her pocket, Sadie again stared out the window, no longer seeing Westwood's mansion but instead her memories of the past. Of her mother, who all her life Sadie had assumed had died in the hospital of the cancer that had ravaged her.

Would she really have done as her father had implied? Wandered off out into the Alaskan wilderness to die in the snow, rather than die at a hospital or at home, in front of her beloved daughters? It made a terrible kind of sense, but at the same time, would her mother have given up even a minute of life with her children? Sadie's instinct told her no.

Her mother hadn't disappeared.

At least, not voluntarily.

She lay back in her seat, staring at the roof of the truck, her eyelids heavy with both sleep and shock. It was all too much to take in; yet another mystery to pile on yet another load of mysteries.

Why had her father written her mother's name on the map, and why in Inuit? And if the map wasn't leading her to the answers about her sister's death, then what did it lead to?

Had her father killed her mother? Or her sister? Had he killed them both?

Sadie was starting to wonder just how many killers she needed to hunt.

And if one of the victims she really needed to get justice for was herself.

CHAPTER FOURTEEN

Sadie's eyes jolted open at the sudden, piercing noise.

A woman was screaming loudly, and it was a sound of pure terror that momentarily froze Sadie's blood in her veins.

Without stopping to think, Sadie rushed out of the vehicle and toward the house, her hand on the butt of her pistol, ready to draw.

As she reached the front door, she only vaguely registered the fact that she should be surprised that the door was ajar. Instead, she shoved it open, running inside, then stopping dead when she realized that she wasn't inside Westwood's home at all.

Instead, a dark tunnel stretched out in front of her, a dim light coming from somewhere far ahead. As her eyes adjusted to the gloom, she saw that she was inside some kind of cave. Like the cave that her father's map had led her and Cooper to.

The woman's scream came again, louder this time, and Sadie gasped as the sound tore at a long-buried memory within her. She was certain she had heard that scream before. That she recognized that voice…

She forged ahead, making her way toward the dim light, her heart thundering inside her chest. She had to get to the screaming woman, to help her.

To save her.

But the tunnel seemed to go on and on, and even though the woman continued to scream, it didn't sound as though Sadie was getting any nearer to her destination. Neither was the light getting any brighter. The tunnel seemed to go on forever.

"I'm coming!" Sadie yelled, knowing only that she had to get to the screaming woman. Was it Jessica? Or, this time, was it her mother? She ran ahead into the darkness, praying that she would reach the woman before something terrible happened. Before the screaming stopped forever.

She stopped abruptly as the ground fell away beneath her, grabbing the walls of the cave to stop herself from plummeting down into the shaft which had suddenly appeared at her feet.

The screams were coming from deep within the shaft.

"Hold on! I'm coming!" Sadie yelled again. The screaming stopped. But was that because the woman had heard her, or because of something more sinister?

Narrow steps led down into the deep blackness of the shaft, and Sadie could only see the first few steps. She had no idea how deep it was, or what could be waiting for her down there, but she knew she had to go down. She had to reach the woman below whose screams she recognized.

Carefully, she started to lower herself into the shaft, testing the steps carefully. They were wooden and flimsy, bending and creaking beneath her feet, and she could only pray that they would prove to hold her weight. As she descended into the shaft, she left the light behind, until she was going down into complete darkness, moving by feel only on the inadequate steps.

Then suddenly, there were no steps at all. Sadie was falling into darkness, with no idea of when—if ever—she would hit the ground.

She screamed, a long and terrified sound that ripped the breath from her lungs. And as she did so, she realized it was the same scream that had led her into the shaft in the first place….

Sadie's eyes jerked open as the sound of her own scream reverberated around the inside of her truck. She stopped abruptly, sitting straight up in her seat, her breath coming in pants.

It was a dream. Just a dream. But she was covered in a thin sheen of cold sweat, and the hairs on the backs of her arms were raised, the terror from her dream still physically lingering on her body.

Not again, Sadie thought, slumping back into her chair, feeling exhausted in both body and mind. The nightmares had been regular since her arrival back in Alaska, although this one had been different than usual. They generally always featured Jessica, playing on the horror Sadie had always felt over her sister's death and the unfounded but no less powerful guilt that she should have somehow been able to save her.

This dream had been different, no doubt triggered by the news that Cooper had given her, which she knew she wasn't even close to being able to process. It still didn't feel real, and perhaps it wouldn't until she had seen the file on her mother that Cooper had.

Or until she found out just what was waiting for her inside that cave…

A light went on in the porch of Westwood's home and Sadie snapped to attention, putting thoughts of the mysteries surrounding her family to one side, for now at least.

She hunkered down in her seat, covered by the darkness, watching as Westwood came out of his door and walked toward his Jaguar. Light flooded his drive, and she saw with a sinking feeling in her gut that he was dressed in dark clothes, with a scarf wrapped around his face. Of course, that wasn't unlikely at this time of year in Anchorage, but it also made it difficult to identify him.

Just like the man on the camera…

It had to be him, Sadie thought, watching him get into his Jag and pull away. She started her engine and began to follow, keeping a careful distance as they got onto the main road, letting a few other late-night travelers get in between them.

Was he going to meet another victim? Where else would he be going at this time of night, and dressed like that? Like he didn't want to be recognized. But would he really be so stupid as to use the same car, knowing that they were already onto him?

Sadie remembered his cockiness earlier and decided that yes, he probably would. Kent Westwood thought he was untouchable, and the killings had ramped up to the point that he was clearly unable to resist the urge even if it did put him at risk of deception. Those girls' corpses were the work of a sadistic killer who was driven by desires too dark to follow the usual trajectory. The lack of time between Vicky Sable's body and the as yet unidentified victim had shaken Sadie and, she could tell, Detective Linden too.

They had to stop this guy, or the bodies were going to pile up.

Sadie reached for her phone, wondering if she should call O'Hara, or even Linden himself, but then decided against it. It was still possible that Westwood was on his way to nowhere more sinister than the late-night shopping mall. The last thing she needed was to make a fool of herself in front of the old detective, who she strongly suspected would never let her live it down.

She carefully weaved in and out of traffic, making sure that she never lost sight of Westwood but kept enough of a distance that he wouldn't notice the truck following him. They were heading deeper into the heart of the city center and Sadie started to wonder if the late-night shopping mall wasn't actually his destination.

Then he took the turn for the Anchorage train station and Sadie felt a curl of horror in her stomach as she realized her hunch had been right.

He was going to meet someone.

The next victim?

Resisting the urge to speed up and potentially alert Westwood to her presence, Sadie waited until she too came to the turning and then tailed him inside the station. She parked at the drop-off area, where she could see both the vehicle exit and entrance and drummed her fingers on the steering wheel.

Following him inside was too risky; he would no doubt recognize her instantly if he spotted her. But what if she missed him coming back out? She still couldn't believe that he would be quite so stupid as to use the same car to pick up another victim only thirty-six hours after Vicky Sable.

Then her phone rang, and as she pulled it out of her pocket, she saw that it was the police chief.

There was news on the second body.

Keeping her eyes peeled for any sign of Westwood reappearing, Sadie answered the phone.

"Sorry to wake you, Price, but we need you here. I've assembled a task force, headed up by Detective Linden. You and O'Hara will be assisting him."

This is going to be interesting, Sadie thought. "A task force," she repeated. "I take it we have new information?"

"The victim has been identified as Rose Perez. Another student at Anchorage City College."

Sadie felt her stomach roll. Another young woman on the cusp of life, only to have it cut short.

"Any connection to Vicky Sable? Were they friends?"

"Not that we know of…yet. So far, the only link is they were all students at the college. But that's enough to start with."

"Anything on the identity of the killer?"

"Nothing," the chief said, sounding frustrated. "But you can probably rule Westwood out."

"Rule him out?" Sadie decided it was a good time to let him know where she was. "I've just tailed him to the train station. Dressed much like he was in the video from the bus station. I think he might be meeting his next victim. You might want to get Detective Linden over here. I'll call Agent O'Hara."

"Aren't you listening?" The chief sounded angry. "The time of death is just before sunset. It rules Westwood out. I need you to work with the task force, Agent Price, not go maverick on us."

“Time of death isn’t an exact science,” Sadie argued, ignoring his last comment. She guessed her reputation preceded her. “He had time to do it and get back and changed before Detective Linden and I showed up.”

“He has an alibi for both murders,” the chief pointed out. “We have nothing on him. And he’s an important figure in this town. You start harassing him without just cause and he’ll be suing our asses.”

“I’m FBI,” Sadie pointed out. “He can’t sue you.” Not that she suspected ASAC Golightly would be any happier right now if it was him on the other end of this call. Sadie shifted impatiently in her seat. Westwood was up to something; she would bet money on it. And she was sure that with enough time she could crack his alibi.

But she might not have time.

“Agent Price,” the chief continued, “please. We need you at the station, not off on some wild goose chase.”

“I’ll be there,” she said, and hung up before he could pin her down as to exactly when that would be.

Sadie felt torn. She needed to get on that task force and start investigating the most recent murder. She could be wrong about Westwood, and even if she wasn’t, they didn’t have enough on him right now.

Then she saw him driving back out of the station with a young woman sitting next to him in the front seat of the car, and her jaw set with determination. This was all far too timely for Sadie to believe it was all just a coincidence. The man and car on the bus station footage could easily be Westwood, and now here he was, picking up another young woman in similar circumstances.

Then there was the vibe that she had picked up from him. Her instincts screamed that Westwood was a predator, and Sadie had learned to trust her instincts. Even Detective Linden, who she suspected was the type to dismiss her gut feelings as “women’s intuition” or something similar, had agreed. And for all that she disliked the man and disagreed with his interrogation techniques, he hadn’t gotten to be a top detective by being unable to spot a villain when he saw one.

She wished now that she had called him before he had been woken up and put on the task force, because now she had no choice but to tail and potentially confront Westwood on her own. Not that those tactics were new for her, but she didn’t want to be responsible for generating any further hostility between the FBI and the Anchorage police force, or to give herself more of a reputation as a maverick when Internal Investigations were about to render their decision.

But she wasn't about to turn around and leave Westwood on his own with the woman he had just picked up from the train station either. She would rather be wrong and be scorned by everyone around her than be responsible for another body wrapped in plastic and dumped in the old warehouses like so much trash.

Westwood pulled back onto the main road and as before, Sadie waited until there were a couple of vehicles between them before pulling out and starting to follow. Her adrenaline was high and her pulse jumping in her neck as she tailed him, her hands tight on the wheel. Was she about to interrupt a murder?

The chief's refusal to even consider the idea of Westwood's guilt, based on a fuzzy timeline and an obviously shady alibi, bothered Sadie. She knew that Golightly would secretly have her back on this, even if he would chew her out first for not immediately collaborating with the task force. It was obvious that Westwood's money had more of a hold on the powers-that-be in Anchorage than she had been aware of.

Which made her only more determined to take him down. Criminals were criminals, regardless of their bank account. She had more respect for a petty criminal like Scrapper, who was just trying to survive, than the likes of Kent Westwood.

As they approached his mansion the cars between them turned off the main road and fell away. Sadie hung back, hoping that Westwood was distracted enough by the woman in the passenger seat to not notice Sadie's truck and realize that it had been behind him the whole way. When she saw him pull in to park outside his mansion, Sadie continued driving down the main road, giving him time to get in the house without seeing her pull up after him. As she did so she prayed that Westwood wouldn't have already gotten to work before she got inside the house.

She looped around at the end of the stretch and came back on herself, parking just down the road from Westwood's place before getting out of her truck and jogging through the snow toward the front door. The light in the upstairs window was on, as it had been before.

Westwood was in there. With his next victim.

Sadie drew her gun.

CHAPTER FIFTEEN

Sadie paused for a moment outside the door, wondering on her best course of action. She had no warrant and the police chief had made it quite clear that she would need more evidence before she got one. But if she simply knocked on the door, Westwood didn't have to answer it, or let her in if he did.

She knocked anyway, but also took the safety off her gun, ready to shoot the lock off the door. As far as she was concerned there was a potentially immediate risk to life, and that gave her jurisdiction to enter, warrant or no warrant. The Anchorage police chief wasn't her boss.

But before she could shoot, she heard the locks being pulled back on the other side of the door. Lowering her gun, she waited for the door to open, half expecting to see the maid. Instead, it was Westwood himself, peering at her with a puzzled look on his face.

Then he recognized her and gave her a look of indignant fury. "What are you doing here, Agent? It's past midnight."

He was a good actor. Sadie could almost believe his protested innocence if it hadn't been for the micro-expression of fear that had first crossed his face when he realized who she was. He was hiding something.

"I was just passing," Sadie said sweetly. "And I remembered that there are a few things that we didn't ask you earlier."

Westwood wasn't mollified by her tone.

"It's a shame you didn't remember what I told you and your friend," he snapped. "That I have no intention of answering any more questions without a lawyer present."

He went to close the door on her, then frowned as he saw that Sadie's boot was firmly wedged between the door and the frame. He glared at her. "What the hell?"

Sadie lifted her hand slightly, just enough to draw his attention to the gun.

"You need to let me in, Mr. Westwood," she said quietly, "or I'm going to have to let myself in. Is that clear?"

A cold sweat broke out on Kent Westwood's forehead. He looked around outside as though worried what the neighbors might think, then stepped back and let Sadie inside.

He was visibly nervous now, his bravado seeping from him, watching as Sadie looked around and then started to make her way toward the central staircase. Kent quickly placed himself between her and it.

"What do you think you're doing! You can't just barge in here and start walking around like you own the place. You need a warrant! I'm phoning the chief of police." The confidence started to creep back into his expression again. "We're very friendly. I donated a lot of money to local projects last year."

Sadie raised her eyebrows at him. "Is that so? The problem for you, Mr. Westwood, is I couldn't give a damn. I don't work for the Anchorage Police Department, and I'm not scared of you or your money. Now I need to see the young woman you just brought here from the train station, or I will tear this place apart."

She saw Westwood go white at the mention of the woman. "I don't know what you're talking about," he snapped, but he was visibly shaken. Sadie went to walk past him.

"Alright!" He threw his hands up in the air. "I have a young woman here, yes. I have a *date*, Agent, do you know what that is?" He attempted a sneer, but the fear was still obvious in his eyes. Ignoring him, Sadie sidestepped him and started to jog up the stairs.

She needed to find the girl.

Had she given Westwood enough time to kill her? Sadie sped up, taking the stairs two at a time.

And then fell hard on her face as Westwood grabbed her legs from behind and started to pull her down toward him. Sadie whipped around and struck him hard on the side of the head with her pistol, and he tumbled down the sides. Breathing heavily from the shock and impact of the sudden attack, she raced up the rest of the stairs and down the upstairs corridor, throwing doors open as she went.

"FBI!" she yelled. But there was no answer, and no one came out of the rooms. She had reached the final door when she heard Westwood thundering up the stairs again.

I should have hit him harder, she thought grimly, throwing the final door open.

Then she gasped out loud at what she saw in the room before her.

A woman lay spreadeagled on a double bed, handcuffed to the posts by her wrists and ankles. Her dress had been pulled down to reveal her breasts, and up around her waist. Next to her on the bed was an assortment of what Sadie supposed were sex toys, except that they looked more like torture implements than any vibrator she had ever seen.

The woman's eyes were closed and her body limp.

"Hello? Can you hear me?" Sadie ran to her side.

The woman was unconscious. She was about to feel for a pulse when she heard Westwood running into the room behind her. Sadie whirled on him, pointing her gun in the center of his chest.

"Hands in the air," she said coldly, enunciating every word, "or I will shoot you, and my hands aren't feeling very steady right now."

Westwood stared at the gun, then at Sadie's face, saw the absolute truth of her words, and then slumped in defeat, although his eyers glittered at her vengefully. Keeping her gun trained on him, Sadie took out her own handcuffs with one hand. She handcuffed him to the post at the end of the bed, then ran back to the woman, pulling out her radio as she did so.

"I need an ambulance," she said, and listened to the responder's gasp when she gave the address.

"Kent Westwood's house?"

"Yes. Right now. And the police. Detective Linden at the APD."

Then she ended the call, taking a deep breath as she knelt down next to the woman and checked for a pulse, her own heart hammering in her chest at the thought that she was examining a fresh corpse. Then she felt it and gave an audible sigh of relief. The pulse was there, but it was faint. The woman's skin had a waxy sheen to it.

"What have you given to her?" Sadie demanded, looking at Westwood in disgust.

"I haven't given her anything," he protested, although he wasn't meeting her eyes. "She has clearly had too much to drink. She was drunk when I picked her up."

Sadie felt her hand curl into a fist at her side. "You're lying," she said, spitting the words out from between her teeth, "and a toxicology report will show that. Besides, tying up an intoxicated woman isn't much of a defense, especially when you're clearly stone cold sober. I'll ask you again; what did you give her?"

Westwood didn't answer, staring stubbornly at the wall above her head.

"Do you want to go down for murder?" she asked sharply, and Westwood finally looked at her properly, his eyes wide. "If the medics have to waste time figuring out what's wrong with her, she could die."

She saw Westwood swallow, his Adam's apple bobbing in his throat.

"Rohypnol," he said sullenly, unable to meet her eyes again. Sadie's stomach curled. Rohypnol. The date rape drug.

"How much? She's not waking up." Sadie could hear the thread of panic in her own voice. The girl looked like more of a corpse than a living person. What if she had gotten here too late?

"I injected her. In the car," Westwood told her, shame momentarily filling his voice. "I tried to judge the dose, but she reacted a lot quicker than I expected. I practically had to carry her in here."

Sadie cursed herself for being so careful not to be seen. At the time it had been the right thing to do, but had she seen Westwood dragging an unconscious woman out of the car she could have rescued her from his clutches a lot quicker.

She prayed that the ambulance would hurry up.

Because otherwise, it was going to be too late.

CHAPTER SIXTEEN

"Good work, Agent Price," Detective Linden told her as he started to lead a handcuffed and subdued Westwood down the central staircase of his fancy home. Sadie felt pleasantly surprised by the words, even if their delivery sounded somewhat grudging.

Linden was accompanied by Agent O'Hara, who looked rumpled and tired, and another local detective, a slightly overweight guy with a large white mustache. Sadie hadn't liked the way the other detective's eyes had lingered on the half-naked form of the woman on the bed when they had arrived, just moments after the ambulance.

The woman had been taken to the main hospital, with assurances that she was likely to be fine, but it would be a few hours before she was likely to be awake enough for them to take a statement from her.

"I'll take Westwood to the cells," Linden told her. "If you and Agent O'Hara can wait for the forensics team to get here? We need this place turned over."

"There's nothing to find," Westwood protested. "And I won't be cooperating with any interview until my lawyer arrives." With the reality of being caught and arrested now manifest, Westwood's attitude was coming back. Sadie gave him a cool glare. He wouldn't be getting away with any of this, she vowed. Judging by the look of sheer disgust on Linden's face as he had eyed the bedroom where the girl had been trussed up, he felt the same way.

"That's fine by me," Linden said with sarcasm. "You can spend the rest of the night in the cells. You won't be alone. I picked a couple of guys up earlier. Rowdy bikers. Tough guys. I should warn you; they won't like being locked up with a rapist."

Westwood's eyes widened and he looked terrified as Linden dragged him off, the other detective, Regan, in tow. Sadie watched them go and then turned to O'Hara, who let his breath out with a long whistle.

"You don't do things by halves do you?" he said, though he sounded more admiring than admonishing. A rookie, she knew that

O'Hara had been starstruck by her when she had first arrived at Anchorage Field Office.

"I should have called you," she said, "but one of us needed to sleep. I don't know what I was expecting by staking Westwood out, but it certainly wasn't this."

They sat on the bottom step, waiting for the forensics team.

"Do you think they will find anything here to connect him to the murders?" O'Hara asked. He was looking around at the interior of the house, slightly awed.

"Honestly?" Sadie said, hearing the doubt in her tone. "I'm not sure. Could he really be that stupid…and that sure of himself? But if not in here then we will hopefully find something in the car to connect him to Vicky Sable at least."

O'Hara frowned. "You sound like you're doubting yourself," he pointed out. "You've just gotten him dead to rights. Caught in the act. And if there's anything to find, a drop of blood or a single hair, then forensics will find it. That police chief won't keep defending Westwood now."

"I hope not," Sadie agreed, but then she sighed loudly. "It just doesn't seem to make sense. There was no sign on any of the other women that they had been raped or sexually assaulted. He seems to have just stabbed them and wrapped them up. And he drugged them with benzodiazepines according to the tox report, not Rohypnol. Why change his MO now?"

"Maybe he's a date rapist and a killer?" O'Hara suggested.

Sadie shook her head. "I've never heard of them being separated out like this. It goes against everything we know about serial killers, especially those who are sex offenders as well. All of the victims were young, attractive women, whom Westwood clearly likes. Why only choose to rape this one? Killers can evolve their methods, for sure, but not this quickly. The last victim was only found this evening. Westwood must have arranged this rape scenario before then."

She shuddered as she remembered the scene that she had walked into in the bedroom, wondering what would have happened to the woman if Sadie hadn't decided to break ranks and continue tailing Westwood. Would he have killed her? Would she indeed have ended up gutted and wrapped up in plastic? O'Hara could be right. Maybe the other kills had been leading up to this one.

It still didn't make sense to her, but what about sadistic murder ever did make sense, really? Sure, they could study their behavior and psychology and try to infer patterns, but how much could anyone ever really understand about the workings of pure evil?

Westwood had to be the killer, she told herself. That was why she had been following him, after all, because she had known that he was a sadist. She had sensed it in him immediately. Everything else fit; the car, the dark clothes, the picking up women in public places…

The alternative, Sadie realized, was just too horrible to contemplate.

Because if Kent Westwood wasn't the one duping college students into meeting him, then killing them and wrapping up the bodies, then who was? As yet they had no other leads, and nothing to go on except the make of a car.

If it wasn't Westwood, then they had two sadists on their hands. A killer who was stalking the city campus, killing two victims in two days right under everyone's nose, and a real estate mogul who was in fact nothing more than a rapist with some very dark kinks. And potentially a would-be murderer too, as he had clearly been about to rape the woman even knowing that he could have overdosed her.

Sadie felt sick as she tried to take it all in. She was looking forward to interrogating Westwood in a dark kind of way, desperate to wrestle the truth out of him.

Because if they were dealing with two monsters, then one of them was still roaming around free.

*

Even in an unflattering orange jumpsuit, Kent Westwood managed to exude a certain charm. The shame that Sadie had seen in him after she had cuffed him in his mansion was long gone, at least externally. He sat casually opposite Sadie and Detective Linden, only a slight flex of his fingers betraying any tension. His lawyer sat next to him, a sharp-suited All-American-looking guy with a designer leather briefcase, expensive veneers, and a shark-like smile that didn't reach his eyes. *Two peas in a pod*, Sadie thought with a shudder.

The young woman that Westwood had tied to his bed was in the hospital, stable but in no position to give them a statement yet. Her name was Melissa Davies, and she was an intern at a nearby real estate firm, which was likely where she had come across Westwood.

She wasn't a college student. Only her age matched the profile of the three victims wrapped in plastic. As far as they had been able to discover so far, Melissa had no ties to any of the victims, and according to her cousin whom she lived with, she didn't do social media. It was an entirely different profile from the murder victims.

Although she was trying to suspend judgment, Sadie had a sinking feeling that her earlier hunch had been right, and Westwood wasn't their killer, but an entirely different sort of criminal. Yet everyone else, including Linden, seemed to be operating on the basis that they had their guy. Applying the logic of Occam's razor—that the simplest explanation was usually the right one—it made sense. Could there really be two predators stalking central Anchorage, with an identical make of car and a similar build, and a penchant for young women in their late teens or very early twenties? It seemed too horrific to be true.

In Sadie's experience, however, the exact opposite usually turned out to be the case—the more horrific, the more likely it was to have happened.

Detective Linden was tapping his knuckles on the table as he started the tape, his body tense with barely concealed anger. With Westwood's hotshot lawyer present, Sadie suspected that Linden would do his best to rein in his bad cop approach, but she doubted that he would be very successful. It wasn't a persona with Linden; it was his personality.

"Mr. Westwood, can you explain how Ms. Davies came to be tied up and drugged in your home?" Linden barked, going straight in. Westwood blinked in surprise at the question, glancing at his lawyer.

"You're leading my client," his lawyer drawled in a Southern accent.

"So you're saying Ms. Davies wasn't tied up and drugged? You admitted to Agent Price that you had injected her with Rohypnol." Linden demanded, sounding outraged.

Sadie suppressed a smile. There were times when she could appreciate the older detective's abrasiveness, she decided, if not his old-fashioned views on gender roles.

"Ms. Davies consented to be tied up," Westwood said. "There are messages to prove that on my phone. The phone that you guys confiscated," he pointed out, his voice peevish, as though his main concern was their audacity at taking his belongings.

Sadie found herself hoping that he spent a *very* long time in jail.

"Did she consent to be drugged?" The naked look of disgust on Linden's face would have been comical in any other situation.

Westwood looked at his lawyer again, his outward confidence slipping for a moment.

"It was a role-playing scenario," he said. "We had worked out all the details beforehand. It was fully consensual."

"Did she consent to be drugged?" Linden asked again, his voice just a few decibels away from outright yelling.

"I will be making a complaint if you continue to be aggressive to my client, Detective," Westwood's lawyer said silkily.

"You think this is aggressive?" Linden growled. Sadie decided that this would be a good time to step in.

"Special Agent Price, Anchorage FBI," she said coolly. "Mr. Westwood indeed admitted to me that he had injected Ms. Davies with Rohypnol. Otherwise known as the 'date rape drug.' You can claim role-play all you like, but unless you have documented proof of that I suggest you come up with a better defense. Do you really think Ms. Davies is going to corroborate that? Because I don't, and I've met men like you before, Kent. And regardless of whether consent was involved at any point, Rohypnol is a highly illegal drug. You've admitted to a federal crime."

She allowed her complete disdain for the man to show on her face.

"You know what happens to men like you?" she asked him, smiling slightly. "They usually end up in twenty-four-hour isolation in prison. The other inmates don't like sex offenders, you see. Especially not the sort that rape helpless women."

Westwood hadn't moved a muscle and his expression hadn't changed, but Sadie could almost feel the fear radiating from him as she painted the picture of his future life in prison.

"This is disgraceful!" his lawyer spluttered. "You're intimidating my client!"

Sadie shrugged.

"I have a few other questions, Mr. Westwood," she continued, "concerning your activities over the last few days. You seem to make a habit of picking up young women."

Westwood smirked, attempting to regain his bravado, but she could see his hands were shaking slightly in his lap. She knew that Melissa Davies wasn't going to agree with his ludicrous story, and even if she did, it was a legal gray area. You couldn't consent to future events you couldn't possibly be certain of, even if she had taken Rohypnol willingly as some kind of crazy sex game, which Sadie didn't believe for one minute.

"I'm a ladies' man, Agent Price. Is that a crime?"

"Yes it is when you drug and attempt to rape them. And when you kill them and dump their bodies around the city." Her tone was as light as if she were discussing the weather, belying the tension that now permeated the room.

"Why are you asking me about that again?" Westwood protested. "I told you I had nothing to do with any of that."

"This is unacceptable, Agent," his lawyer cut in again. "My client is not here to answer questions about another case."

"Actually," Sadie said, her lips tightening as she looked at the lawyer, wishing she could get away with wiping the smug expression from his face, "yes, he is. I'm investigating that case, along with Detective Linden here, and your client is a suspect. Our main suspect, in fact. It seems like a big coincidence that he is also kidnapping and drugging young women, don't you think? Just how dark do your sexual tastes get, Mr. Westwood?" She raised her eyebrows, directing her last comment at the real estate playboy.

If she had expected her words to put him at a disadvantage, she quickly realized that she had underestimated him. Westwood leaned forward, something dark glittering in his eyes. The way his gaze swept over Sadie made her shudder.

"Would you like to find out, Agent Price?"

Detective Linden slammed his hand down on the table, making everyone else around it jump. "You don't speak to her that way," he snarled. "We're taking a break, Mr. Westwood. You can go and cool your heels in the cells for a bit longer."

"You can't..." the lawyer began, only to be cut off by Detective Linden getting abruptly to his feet. "The hell I can't."

The interrogation was, for the time being, over. Sadie followed Linden out into the corridor, waited for him to finish instructing the young police officer to take Westwood back down to the cells, and then turned to him when they were alone.

"I appreciate what you did in there," she began, "but I can handle Westwood. I've come across worse."

Linden shook his head. "Women in law enforcement are a bad idea," he said to the wall in front of him. "I've always said it and I stand by it. We end up wasting our time protecting you all from the likes of that slime bag in there."

Sadie felt exasperated as she shook her head. "I don't need protecting, Detective. And especially not from Westwood."

"I bet Melissa Davies thought the same thing," Linden snapped.

Sadie swallowed down her retort about the victim not being a seasoned FBI agent and took a deep breath, trying to find some compassion for the fierce older detective. He meant well, she thought, even if his views on the sexes wouldn't have been out of place back in Victorian Britain. She also suspected his failure to solve Roxie's death was weighing heavier on him as more victims continued to up.

"Okay," she said, taking a deep breath. "We should probably leave questioning him again until we have a statement from Ms. Davies and the forensics report from his mansion, computer, and car. I've got O'Hara tracking down any other Jaguars in the areas around Anchorage, including from rental car firms. Something will show up, and we'll get him."

"We'll get him for Davies," Linden said, clearly beginning to think along the same lines as Sadie, "but what ties him to the other victims? We won't get a confession out of him, especially not with that lawyer around."

"Hopefully, we won't need one," Sadie said quietly. "Let's get back to the task force."

Something would shake loose, she told herself, something that would lead them straight to the killer.

It had to.

CHAPTER SEVENTEEN

A meeting room at the station had been swiftly turned into the room for the task force, and Sadie walked in to find the team already assembled. Agent O'Hara was there, looking exhausted, as well as the overweight older guy, Detective Boyd, who had been at the mansion with Linden. She wondered if he was his regular partner. There were also three other junior detectives, all fresh-faced and eager to learn. She guessed this was their first serial killer case.

They were all male, too, even though she knew there were plenty of females in the Anchorage Police Department. She wondered if the chief had done that deliberately to appease Linden and felt angry at the thought. The detective needed dragging into the twenty-first century before his attitudes compromised the case, she thought.

It also meant she was the only female on the task force, and she thoroughly expected Linden to try to sideline her. She was surprised then, when after giving the group a rundown of what they knew—or rather, didn't know—so far, he asked Sadie to come to the front to talk to the rest of them.

"Agent Price is an expert at the FBI Behavioral Analysis Unit," he said, albeit grudgingly. "She has worked a few of these sorts of cases. What can you tell us about the type of man this guy is, Price?" His words sounded like a challenge, one that he expected her to fail, and Sadie felt uncharacteristically under pressure as she stood up and made her way to the front of the room, standing in front of the whiteboard where large pictures of the three victims were now pinned, smiling out across the room.

"Okay," Sadie said, noticing the rapt attention on the faces of the other detectives, especially Boyd, who was leaning forward in his chair to listen to her, "the first thing to know is behavioral analysis isn't an exact science. Although we use data modeling as well as what we know of criminal psychology, the sorts of people who commit serial murder aren't exactly what you would call the norm. They're anomalies, if you like, although we do see some distinct patterns."

She glanced back at the pictures of the victims, noticing sadly how fresh-faced and young all three women looked. "The most obvious thing here is our guy is targeting young women, all students so far. Practically that indicates a link to the college, of course, but it's also worth thinking about what attracts him to this particular demographic in the first place, as his choice is unlikely to be purely opportunistic."

She paused, waiting to see if any of the detectives offered the obvious answer.

"Sex," Styles said. The others nodded.

"You would think so," Sadie said, "but the almost odd thing about these killings is there is no sign of sexual interference with the victims. Of course, that doesn't mean he isn't getting some form of sexual gratification from the act, but these aren't primarily sexually motivated murders."

"So, what, he just likes the act of killing?" O'Hara asked.

"Possibly. With serial killers, we tend to see two obvious categories, although they aren't always mutually exclusive. Process killers and product killers. Process killers, as the name implies, are interested in the lead-up to the kill and the kill itself. They get gratification from choosing their victim, possibly stalking them, and possibly torturing them. They will likely have been fantasizing about killing for a long time before they actually do it, and you tend to see an escalation. Especially with sex offenders, who may start off with sexual assault and rape before moving on to killing."

She briefly met Linden's eyes, thinking of Westwood. Detective Linden was listening in spite of himself, with not an eye roll or disbelieving snort in sight.

"Product killers are a lot less interested in the build-up to the kill, and even the kill itself, than what they can take from it. There may be a strong interest in the actual body, such as in the case of necrophiliac or cannibalistic killers."

The faces in front of her looked queasy.

"So, we're looking at a process killer?" Linden asked.

"To a large degree, yes," Sadie agreed. "If 'Brett' is an indication of how he's meeting his targets, then there's an obvious process of targeting and grooming before he finally meets and kills them, even if the way he kills them is in itself quite swift—there were no signs of torture on any of the victims. But the fact he kills them in such an odd way, and in the same way each time, would suggest he is getting a lot of satisfaction from it. It's ritualized behavior.

"However," she added, "I think we're seeing some elements of 'product' killing here, too. The way he wraps them in plastic, and so carefully, makes me think this is the main part of it for him. That's the part he's getting off on the most. Although he's dumping the bodies pretty quickly, I wouldn't be surprised if he's taking photographs of them."

The other young detective, sitting next to Styles, shook his head in disbelief. "It's weird," he said. "Have you ever come across something like this before?"

"Not quite," Sadie acknowledged, "but I think it's fairly obvious where this particular fetish comes from. He's a fisherman, or a fishmonger, or something similar."

Linden nodded slowly. "The smell of fish on the bodies," he said. "I thought it was because he had killed them near the wharf, but when you think about how he's killed them…"

"Gutted them like fish," O'Hara cut in, his mouth twisted in disgust, "and then packaged them up like fillets."

"Exactly," Sadie said.

"But why?" Styles said, looking confused. "Why is he treating them like fish? That's just insane."

"That's what we don't know, and whatever his reasons are, they might not make any kind of logical sense to us. The point is, they do to him. Men who target young women like this are often misogynists and as Styles pointed out, often sexually motivated, but I don't think that's what is going on here, not exactly. He's dehumanizing them, stripping them of their humanity and comparing them to animals that we tend to think of as cold-blooded and devoid of personality. That speaks more to me of an inability to empathize than hatred or resentment. I think we will find that our guy isn't particularly good with women. He may even avoid them."

As she spoke, Sadie realized that the hypothetical killer that she was describing was the exact opposite of Kent Westwood. The chief was right; the real estate playboy wasn't the one.

Sadie made her way back to her seat, leaving them to digest her insights.

"That was interesting," Linden said, his tone making it clear that his own interest had surprised him. "But I bet it wasn't all that academic knowledge that helped you track down the Boston Mangler, was it? That's not what I heard. Good old-fashioned policing, that was."

Unsure if she was supposed to take that as a compliment or an insult, Sadie decided not to respond, taking her seat back next to Agent O'Hara, who shot her a tired look of sympathy. O'Hara had the gray pallor and dilated pupils of someone who had too much coffee and not enough sleep.

"Okay," Linden said, clearing his throat, "it's nearly morning. Let's make ourselves useful while we wait for forensic evidence to come back to us. Agent O'Hara and Detective Styles, I want you both to go down to the college campus and see if we have any witnesses to Perez's last movements other than her roommates. Hang around, see if there is any gossip flying around about any of the victims. Especially their online behavior. Someone must know something."

The detective nodded, looking pleased to be assigned a task, but O'Hara looked less than pleased.

"I'm not his lackey to order about," he murmured to Sadie.

"No, but let's keep him sweet for now until we know more," Sadie whispered back. She was expecting Linden to assign the other detective and Boyd a task and for the two of them to be speaking to Perez's family, so she wasn't expecting his next words.

"Detective Green, you can come with me to speak to the Perez family. Boyd, go with Agent Price to speak to Perez's roommates. Get hold of all of her internet devices. Let's see if 'Brett' makes another appearance."

The IT analysts still hadn't been able to track Brett down. Whoever he was, he had some impressive cyber skills.

Sadie felt her face go warm at the way Linden spoke to her as though she was one of his detectives, or even a junior agent like O'Hara. He might be the head of the task force, but he wasn't her superior and sooner or later she was going to have to again make that clear to him.

Now, however, wasn't the time. Instead, she nodded sharply and grabbed her parka, ignoring Detective Boyd's grin as he followed her out of the room. She had him pegged as a sleazy old guy, and the sooner this particular task was over, the better.

They took his patrol car, which smelled of tobacco and something else, a faint undercurrent that seemed familiar, and recently so, but that Sadie couldn't quite place.

"We'll stop for a coffee and some pancakes at the diner," Boyd said, patting his too-large belly as he made himself comfortable in the driver's seat, "and we should get to the campus at about the right time.

No sense in waking them up too early, you know what young girls are like."

Sadie didn't. At college she had been driven and studious, determined to work hard and achieve her ambitions of getting into Quantico and getting away from her past for good.

That hadn't turned out so well. She pushed the thoughts of Sheriff Cooper's revelations—and the full horror of their implications—out of her mind. She couldn't concentrate on this case while also thinking about her sister's and now potentially her mother's murders and her father's potential involvement. The fact that her entire history appeared to have been a lie. Sadie was good at compartmentalizing—she had to be in her occupation—but recently she was starting to become more and more frayed at the edges. Things were getting on top of her.

"You okay?" Boyd asked as he pulled away from the station. "This case getting to you, is it?" He glanced at her sympathetically.

"No," Sadie said shortly. "I've worked a lot worse."

"Yeah, the Mangler. I've heard about that. You killed him, didn't you?"

"Yes," she said, even shorter. "He was about to kill me."

"Hey, it wasn't a criticism," Boyd protested, sounding surprised at her response. "The guy deserved to die. I remember reading about it in the paper. Real sicko, wasn't he?"

"One of the worst," Sadie agreed quietly. The Mangler had earned his epithet from the state of his victims' bodies after he had finished torturing them to death. It wasn't a case that Sadie was ever likely to forget.

It might well be the case that finished her career, depending on the final decision from Internal Investigations. Something else that she was desperately trying not to think about.

Sadie shook her head to clear it. Stress was piling up on her and the lack of sleep wasn't helping.

"Coffee and pancakes actually sounds great," she said.

"Girl after my own heart." Boyd grinned. "Got a boyfriend?"

Sadie thought about Cooper. "Yes," she said, wondering if that was true. Was he her boyfriend? Did she want him to be? That could go on her list of things to be dealt with another time, too.

"Can't blame a guy for trying," Boyd said cheerfully. Sadie looked out the window and rolled her eyes, hoping Linden wasn't going to assign Boyd to her for the rest of this case. Perhaps he thought the old detective would protect her, she thought wryly.

Sadie continued staring out the window, hoping that Boyd would be quiet for the rest of the journey, but that turned out to be wishful thinking.

"You know, I'm surprised we don't have more gruesome murders in Alaska."

"Why's that?" Sadie asked dully.

"Well, look at it." Boyd took a pudgy hand off the steering wheel and waved it at the windshield. "It's so dark, all the time. Here we are coming up to spring, and we are still only getting a few hours of full sunlight at best."

Sadie looked at him, puzzled. "I'm not making the connection," she said.

"Well, isn't it obvious? People go crazy in the dark, don't they? You hear about all the suicides and depression people get when there's not enough sun, it must work the same way with people who harbor violent thoughts or dark fantasies. I mean, the clue is in the name, right?"

Sadie shook her head. Boyd sounded enthusiastic about his theory and reminded her more of a true crime fan than an actual detective who should know better, theoretically anyway.

Killers would kill whatever the weather.

"Think about it," Boyd continued, either not noticing or not caring about Sadie's lack of enthusiasm on the subject, "there are more places to hide in the dark, more opportunities to get away with things unseen, and there's all the horror stories about things coming out in the dark, monsters under the bed and all that. Maybe they're all based on the fact that deep down, we know the dark really is dangerous."

He paused and Sadie realized he was staring at her, waiting for a response.

"Interesting theory," she said, more in the hope he would turn his eyes back to the icy roads they were driving on rather than a wish to continue the conversation. Boyd was an oddball, she thought, remembering how he had leaned forward, listening intently, during her talk in the task force room.

At least someone had been impressed. She was surprised that Detective Linden hadn't openly rolled his eyes and suspected that he had asked her to speak only to give himself proof of her incompetence.

She wondered vaguely if Linden was jealous. Although Sadie found her status as something of a local hero deeply embarrassing, she was proud of her track record of solving difficult cases. Being outperformed by a younger woman must be needling Detective linden pretty hard.

"Here's the diner." Boyd pulled over sharply outside a rundown little place that looked as though it probably had rats. Then Sadie's belly rumbled audibly, and she decided she didn't care. She could happily eat a rat; she hadn't eaten for hours.

She waited inside the car, looking out at the deserted road and wondering about what Boyd had said. Statistically, he was wrong, but could it be a factor for this killer? Something had to have made him not kill—that they knew of—for six months only to suddenly escalate to two victims in two days. Could the time of year be a factor?

He could have been out of town. Or in prison, she thought.

Then she thought about the fact that both Roxie and Vicky had been about to drop out, and a thought occurred to her. Roxie had dropped out toward the end of the year, Vicky halfway through…

What if there had been no murders in between because there had been no dropouts? From June to August was the holidays, and the fall term was the start of the school year, when dropping out was surely less likely. Could that be the link?

Excited, Sadie pulled out her phone and messaged both O'Hara and Linden with her hunch. They needed to know if Rose Perez had been about to drop out too. If she had, then they had a definite link.

And they needed to find out just who at the college handled that.

It also looked more likely that Westwood was off the hook, Sadie thought, but she was feeling less and less surprised about that prospect. Her instincts that Westwood was a predator had been right—he just hadn't been the predator they had been looking for.

Even so, she wasn't about to entirely rule him out until she had to.

Detective Boyd came back to the car, and the smell of bacon, maple syrup, and coffee made Sadie's stomach grumble noisily again. "Thank you," she said gratefully, tucking into some of the best bacon she had ever tasted.

"So, what do you think?" Boyd asked.

"They're great."

"Not the pancakes. My theory."

This again. Sadie swallowed a mouthful of pancake. "There's no evidence to suggest you're right," she told him. "In fact, as winters have been getting milder in some areas due to climate change, crime has actually gone up in those places. It's one of those things that sounds right, but probably isn't."

Boyd looked disappointed. “Well, I don’t buy that,” he said. “What does some university guy gathering statistics know? I’m telling you that we always have more murders in the winter, especially midwinter when it’s dark most of the time.”

“Really?” Sadie asked, remembering with a shudder her first case when she had arrived back in Alaska at the Midwinter Solstice. It had involved questioning some of the residents of the Inuit village, which was never received well as they had their own law enforcement.

Inuit…the Inuit letters on her father’s map…what the hell was that all about?

Mother Dawn.

She snapped back to the present, realizing that Boyd was speaking again.

“Winter Solstice eighty-six,” he was saying in between mouthfuls of pancake, his voice almost dreamy. “You remember that? That guy who killed, cooked, and ate his own wife?”

“No,” Sadie said, feeling sick as she bit into a particularly gristly bit of bacon. “I wasn’t born, Boyd.”

“New cop, I was. First murder I had ever dealt with. Pleasant guy, everyone liked him, and he just snapped one day, on the shortest and darkest day of the year. There’s got to be a link, don’t you think?”

“I doubt it,” she said in a brisk tone, ignoring Boyd’s crestfallen face as she swigged the last of her coffee. “Let’s get going, shall we?”

Muttering to himself, Boyd drove off, and Sadie tried not to think any further about cannibal killers.

She had enough killers to deal with right now.

CHAPTER EIGHTEEN

Rose's roommate was a thin, pink-haired girl named Marla, with purple horn-rimmed glasses and a colorful tattoo of a rainbow across her neck. She eyed Sadie and Detective Boyd warily, her arms crossed over her chest in a clearly defensive gesture, answering their preliminary questions with a shrug.

"We weren't best friends," she said. "I don't know much about Rose's life. We had different classes and a different social circle. She hung around with the jocks, mostly."

"No boyfriend?" Sadie asked, scanning the room. Marla shook her head.

"Nah. Not on campus anyway. She had one back home, but they broke up a few months ago."

"Do you know why?"

Marla didn't reply, looking defensive again as she sat down at her desk with her arms still folded.

"Did they have a lovers' tiff?" Boyd asked. He was standing by the window, gazing out across the campus intently, and Sadie wondered what he was looking at.

Marla flicked Boyd a charged look, one filled with disdain and… something else. Sadie frowned and wondered if they had met before. There was a distinct smell of marijuana in the room, and she wondered if Boyd had ever picked Marla up for possession. She seemed extra prickly around him, but Boyd showed no sign of recognizing her. Sadie made a mental note to ask him later.

"I think he was really controlling. He didn't trust her living on campus. Ironic really because she only started partying hard after they split up."

"Did she get in with a bad crowd then, do you think? Any arguments with anyone?"

"No," Marla snapped. "There's nothing wrong with partying. There was nothing that she told me about, anyway."

Marla didn't seem particularly upset by the news, Sadie noticed, only by their intrusion into her space. Maybe she and Rose really weren't close…or maybe it was something else.

"When was the last time you saw Rose?"

"Yesterday morning. She was on her way out, she didn't tell me where. I was wasted, to be honest with you, I had been in my boyfriend's dorm all night. There were a few of us there."

"I'll need to corroborate that with your boyfriend and his friends," Sadie said, watching her reaction.

Marla shrugged, seemingly unperturbed. "Sure."

"You said that Rose was partying a lot," Sadie went on. "Was she thinking of dropping out, do you know?"

Marla tipped her head to one side, giving Sadie's question some genuine consideration.

"She didn't tell me if she was, but I wouldn't be surprised; she seemed to spend more time partying or online than going to class. You can ask Student Services; they deal with withdrawals."

"We will. You said she was online a lot?"

Marla nodded, motioning toward Rose's desk with her hand. "Her laptop is over there."

Sadie crossed over to it and opened it up, but unlike Vicky, Rose had carefully passworded her device. It would need to be handed over to the IT forensics. Sadie cursed under her breath.

Then Detective Boyd surprised her by being more social media savvy than she would have expected.

"Are you on Facebook, Marla?"

Marla nodded, looking wary again. In fact, she seemed to flinch under Boyd's gaze. There was definitely something going on here, she thought, or perhaps Marla just had reason to be scared of cops—or men—in general.

"Yeah. Why?"

"Were you friends with Rose on there?"

As Marla nodded, Sadie understood where Boyd's line of questioning was going. If Marla was friends with Rose, they might be able to see Rose's friends list from Marla's profile. "Could you go on to your profile for us and show us Rose's?" Sadie asked, feeling the adrenaline rise in her veins. Brett could be their best chance of tracking the killer down. Their IT experts had to trace him eventually. Even if he was using an internet café, it was a start. Sadie was painfully aware that with Westwood out of the picture all they had left to go on was the make of a car and the smell of fish.

Marla logged in to Facebook on her phone and brought up Rose's profile. Pictures of Rose at various college parties filled her feed. She seemed drunk or high in most of them. So, the girl was a risk-taker, someone who liked to have fun. Maybe even had a self-destructive streak, as that couldn't be helping her education prospects. Exactly the sort of girl, Sadie guessed, who could be persuaded to meet a stranger, even right after another girl from the same campus had just been murdered.

"Can you get on to her friends list?" Sadie asked, holding her breath. Boyd had crossed over the room and was standing behind her, leaning over her shoulder. He didn't smell great, Sadie thought, wrinkling her nose. He smelled of bacon and sweat and engine oil, and something else, an undercurrent that she couldn't quite put her finger on amidst the other odors that permeated the air around him.

"There we go," Sadie murmured, as "Brett" made an appearance on Rose's friends list. The sooner they could get into Rose's laptop, the better.

"Who's that hottie?" Marla asked appreciatively as Sadie asked her to stop on Brett's picture. When neither Sadie nor Boyd answered her, her eyes widened in horror. "Oh my god, are you saying he's the killer?"

"Do you know him?"

"No," Marla said with certainty. "He's not from around here. He would be the talk of the campus if he was."

"And Rose never mentioned him to you?"

"No." Marla sighed, as if in regret. "I told you, we were roommates, but we weren't great friends. We didn't have much in common. I wish I had made more of an effort with her now…" Her voice trailed off and the girl showed genuine upset for her roommate for the first time. Sadie laid a brief hand on her shoulder.

"There was nothing you could have done," she said softly. "We'll leave you to it—for now. But if you think of anything that you haven't told us, even if you don't think it's relevant, please give us a call."

"Can I call you direct?" Marla asked, looking Sadie dead in her eyes.

"Of course," Sadie said, surprised. She handed Marla a card, watching as the girl pocketed it in her jeans. There was something that she wanted to tell her, she thought, but that she didn't want Boyd to hear. "Call me anytime you want."

As they walked back across the campus, Sadie headed for Student Services before they made their way back to Boyd's vehicle. The office was still shut, and didn't open until ten a.m., which was over two hours away. Sadie sighed in frustration.

"It could just be coincidence that they were all about to drop out," Boyd said. "And we don't even know if Perez was."

"There's too many coincidences in this case," Sadie said, thinking of Westwood again, "and in my experience they are usually anything but."

"We'll come back when they're open," Boyd reassured her. "Let's get this laptop back and see what we can find out about our friend Brett."

Sadie nodded and followed him back to the car, then decided to ask him the question that had been niggling at her ever since they had left Marla's room.

"Boyd, have you met Marla before? Even arrested her, maybe? She seemed like she recognized you from somewhere, and wherever it was, I don't think she had fond memories of you."

Boyd looked surprised and then seemed to think seriously about Sadie's question. "No," he said eventually. "Not that I can recall. We could check to see if she's got a record?"

"No need," Sadie said lightly, deciding to do that anyway, even though Boyd's answer had seemed genuine.

As they pulled away from the campus, however, Sadie realized what the undercurrent of odor was that she was picking up from Boyd other than his general smell.

It was fish.

CHAPTER NINETEEN

Sadie returned to the task force room to news that she had been expecting.

"Agent Price." Linden nodded at her as she walked in. "Nothing was found at Westwood's place, or in his car, to incriminate him in the murders. So he won't be going back on our suspect list."

Sadie nodded. "I guess we expected that. I suppose his alibis still hold?"

"Yes, but we've got him for Davies. She's woken up and given a full statement. Along with yours, we've got Westwood for kidnapping and rape. You were right to continue checking him out. The chief owes you an apology."

Sadie's mouth fell open at the gruff praise, and she was about to say thank you when Linden walked off toward the board at the front of the room, clapping his hand for the other detectives to listen. O'Hara stood at the back of the room, leaning against the wall with a coffee in his hand, and Sadie joined him.

"Perez's parents couldn't tell us much," Linden began, clearing his throat. "Seems Rose hadn't been in touch for a while. The mother has been worried that she was partying too much, but they didn't know whether Rose had plans to drop out or not. Apparently, there was a break-up with a boyfriend a few months ago. We checked his address but there was no one home, so we'll try again this afternoon. Of course, usually in these cases he would be one of the chief suspects."

"Did the parents have an alibi?" Sadie asked. Linden nodded curtly, as though annoyed that she had asked.

"We got nothing," O'Hara said, "other than some very annoyed students who didn't want to be woken up."

All eyes swiveled to Sadie.

"We spoke to her roommate, Marla," Sadie told them, "and there's definitely a pattern emerging here. Rose has been partying as the mother says, although Marla isn't in the same social circle, so we'll need to speak to Rose's friends to find out more. Rose couldn't corroborate whether Rose was dropping out or had a new boyfriend.

She did tell us, however, that Rose had been online a lot. And although I couldn't get into her computer, Rose was friends with 'Brett.' I've just dropped the laptop into forensics. To be honest, our best hope of a solid lead is the IT guys tracing 'Brett.' We don't have access to Roxie's phone, but I'm willing to bet we would find Brett on there too."

"Anything to add, Detective Boyd?" Linden said, seeming almost angry that Sadie had found out so much more than he had. The guy was mercurial, Sadie thought, competing with her one minute, dismissing her as a woman the next, and then occasionally heaping praise on her.

He clearly needed therapy around his issues with women.

The thought gave her a jolt, and for a moment she found herself looking at him through narrowed eyes. Did Linden fit the profile of the killer? He certainly showed signs of misogyny, and she suspected there was a lot that went on inside that head that very few people ever found out about.

Stop it, Sadie reprimanded herself, *you're suspecting everyone*. She had spent the ride back surreptitiously taking deep inhales in Boyd's car, trying to detect if the smell really was a fish one, before concluding that she couldn't be entirely sure that she wasn't just imagining things because it was at the forefront of her mind. And after all, there weren't many men in Alaska who didn't go fishing to some degree. If she was going to haul in everyone with a lingering smell of Alaskan cod, then she was going to have a very long list of suspects.

"Nope," Boyd said, happy to let Sadie keep the limelight. "That was about all of it, right enough."

"We'll go back shortly and speak to Student Services," Sadie added. "So far, the only real link between the victims could be that they were all about to drop out."

"But what does that signify?" Detective Styles asked, looking puzzled. "Some kind of vendetta against college dropouts? That makes no sense."

"I'm sure Agent Price can come up with a suitable psychological theory to explain that," Linden cut in. Sadie glared at him, but the detective's expression was carefully neutral.

"A teacher or professor," Agent O'Hara said. "We need the girls' schedules. Do they have a shared teacher?"

"Or their student counselor," Sadie agreed. "Who I suspect we will find at Student Services."

Linden nodded. "I think we need to go with the theory that killer is—or has been—on campus," he said. "And then cast the net wider only if that doesn't work out. Agent O'Hara, are there any updates on the model of car from the footage?"

"There are two rental places that have that model, we're waiting on their records, and three in surrounding areas," he said. "I was planning on interviewing them all today."

Linden looked annoyed again, and Sadie knew it wasn't just her he had a problem with, but the fact that she and O'Hara weren't under his orders.

"You can take Styles with you," Linden barked. "Detective Boyd, stick with Agent Price today. I'm going down to IT to get those guys moving."

He left the room, his back ramrod straight and his brow heavily creased. *The pressure's getting to him*, Sadie thought. She looked at O'Hara and they shared a sympathetic look.

"At least we don't have to deal with him all day again," he murmured. "He grates on my last nerve."

"He feels threatened by us," Sadie whispered back. "Trust me, you'll have worse run-ins with local cops than this."

"You and Sheriff Cooper seem to get along," he said innocently, although Sadie felt herself grow warm at the mention of Cooper.

"We didn't at the beginning," she told the younger agent. "And his sister, the deputy, pretty much hated me. Our first case was disturbing enough that it thawed things out between us."

"The Iceman." O'Hara nodded, referring to Sadie's first case back in Alaska, and the one that had quickly propelled her to the status of local hero.

"Yeah. I wonder what they'll dub this guy."

Sadie left the room and was on the way to the cafeteria to grab a coffee—the stronger the better—when her phone rang in her pocket. She was surprised when she heard Marla's voice on the other end of the phone.

"Agent Price," the girl whispered in a voice that Sadie could only describe as frightened, "there's something that I need to tell you."

Sadie felt a prickle of anticipation go down her spine. This sounded important. "We'll be on our way back over to campus soon," she told the girl. "We'll come and see you first."

"No!" Marla said quickly. "I mean, no 'we.' You can't bring that other guy with you."

"Detective Boyd?" Sadie hesitated, remembering Marla's reaction to the cop. "That's absolutely fine. Would you rather I bring another woman?" she asked, wondering if what Marla was about to reveal was delicate.

"No one from the police," Marla said. "Please. Just you."

"Okay," Sadie agreed. "I'll come now."

She hung up the phone and swigged her coffee, wondering if she should let Linden know, if only to explain why she was about to dash off without Detective Boyd. But something told her not to, that Linden would only insist on coming himself rather than let Sadie take the credit for another fresh lead. And then Marla would clam up and refuse to talk. No, she needed to do this one alone. She could explain to Detective Boyd afterwards.

Unless, she thought with a shudder, remembering the faint, barely there smell of fish in the police car, there was a very good reason why Detective Boyd couldn't be present for whatever it was that Marla wanted to reveal.

Sadie hurried out to her own truck, pulling her parka tightly round herself as the cold air hit her, freezing the tip of her nose. They were heading for another cold spell, she thought, and just in time for spring.

She remembered Boyd's theory on how the darkness turned people mad and increased murders and remembered just how eager he had been about the subject, how he had relished the prospect of telling her about the Solstice '86 killer. Had he been too eager? Sadie wondered now. Had he relished the thought of a killer in the darkness a little too much? After all, it was rare for a cop to carry on like a true crime fan; most of them were too jaded. They saw the reality up close and personal.

Sadie took a deep breath as she started the engine, wondering just what she was about to find out. And whether she would soon be telling Detective Linden that he needed to question one of his own.

CHAPTER TWENTY

Sadie's boots crunched across the frost as she made her way across campus and back toward Marla's dorm block. She knocked on the door lightly and heard Marla moving around within the room, making snuffling sounds. Her eyes were red-rimmed when she opened the door. The news had obviously sunk in about Rose's murder, and the girl looked as though all the energy had drained from her.

"Come in," she said, not meeting Sadie's eyes, waving her inside the room. Sadie entered and sat in a chair near the window, waiting while Marla knelt on her bed, pulling a blanket around her shoulders and blowing her nose with a well-used piece of tissue.

"I'm sorry," Marla said between snorts. "After you left, it just really hit me, you know? Rose is dead. Like, actually dead."

Sadie just nodded, waiting for the girl to come out with whatever was on her mind. There was a silence, during which Marla wrung the tissue in her hands, staring down at her bed. She looked very frail and very young, and Sadie thought with a pang how the victims were only a few years away from being children, and how if there was any justice in the world, they should have had their whole lives in front of them.

She knew, too, that this experience would scar Marla. That the young woman would never look at the world in quite the same way again. Would never have the privilege of believing it to be a safe space again.

"So, what did you want to tell me, Marla?" Sadie asked eventually, trying to hide her impatience, knowing that if she pushed the girl then she might just clam up.

"You won't go back and tell that guy who was with you before?" Marla asked. She looked scared, Sadie thought, and her earlier hunch came back to her—whatever Marla wanted to tell her, it was directly related to Detective Boyd.

"Detective Boyd," Sadie confirmed.

"He's your partner?" Marla asked, looking worried again. Sadie shook her head, reassuring her.

"No. I'm a federal agent. We're working together with the local police on this case, but today is actually the first time I've ever worked with Detective Boyd."

Marla looked relieved, taking a deep breath before she started to speak. "Okay. I didn't know he had become a cop. He used to be security here, up until a few months ago."

Sadie felt confused. "Detective Boyd? You're saying that he worked as security here, on campus?"

"Yeah," Marla said. "He was already here when we started in September. He was on the night shift a lot…but he gave us the creeps."

Sadie tried to absorb the information, which made no sense to her. Detective Boyd had spoken about being a cop back in '86, hadn't he? There was no way that he could have recently joined the force at his age. Could he have left and come back?

"Are you absolutely sure it was Detective Boyd?" Sadie pressed, feeling certain that Marla must have made a mistake. After all, it was dark at night. It would be easy to confuse two men in uniform who perhaps looked vaguely alike. But Marla shook her head adamantly.

"Completely sure. He came in here one night to fix our window, because there was a really bad storm, and the glass blew. And it said 'Boyd' on his badge."

Okay, so it had to be him, Sadie acknowledged. She would have to check his career history back at the station.

"So, what was the problem with him?" Sadie asked, leaning forward in her seat. "You said he gave you the creeps—was that just a feeling, or was there a reason for that?"

"It was a bit of both, really," Marla said. "There was never anything that he did or said that we could complain about, but he just…he seemed to hang around the girls' windows a lot. It wasn't just me and Rose who thought it, some of the other girls on the ground floor said the same thing. It was just a joke really, that he was a Peeping Tom, but me and Rose found it really creepy. I even started thinking that he had broken the window on purpose just so he had an excuse to come in here."

Sadie nibbled on her lower lip as she thought about the implications of what Marla was saying. "Did Detective Boyd ever frighten Rose on any other occasion? Did she mention anything to you?"

Marla looked up, her eyes widening. "You don't think it was him who killed her, do you?" Her already pale face drained of color. Sadie bit back her natural inclination to defend Boyd on the basis of him being a fellow law enforcement officer. She knew better than to assume that cops couldn't be criminals too. Instead, she regarded Marla with a steady gaze, watching the girl's reactions.

"Do you, Marla?" she asked quietly.

"I don't know," Marla whispered. "I just wanted to tell you that we both thought he was creepy. We never thought he was like, an actual killer or anything, but now.... well, I was just shocked when he walked in here."

Sadie nodded. "I understand. And I'll check this out, without revealing that the information came from you. Okay?"

Marla nodded, looking relieved. Was she really that scared of Detective Boyd?

Her friend had just been murdered, Sadie reminded herself. Marla was probably scared of her own shadow right now. And if what she said about Boyd was true…

Sadie stood up, her head whirling with all the unanswered questions that she now had around this case. "Are you sure there's nothing else, Marla? Anything you've remembered since we spoke earlier?"

Marla shook her head. "No. Only, like I said, she seemed to be online a lot. When she was here, anyway. We didn't talk all that much, for roommates. Maybe if I had gotten to know her better…"

Sadie laid a soft hand briefly on Marla's shoulder as she headed to the door. "It wasn't your fault," she told the girl. "The only one to blame is the perpetrator."

Marla looked up at her, suddenly appearing very young, her eyes hopeful.

"You will catch him, won't you?"

Sadie said the word she knew she should never say, the one guarantee that she was always told to never give.

"Yes," she said without hesitation.

As she left the dorm room, she swore to herself that she wasn't going to rest until she had done just that.

It was mid-morning now, so Sadie headed down to Student Services, weaving through college kids hanging around chatting or on their way to classes. They looked at her curiously, some of them shrinking away when they saw her badge. The atmosphere was subdued, and Sadie guessed that the news about both Vicky and Rose would soon be known all over campus. The young women would no doubt be warned not to wander around on their own, and to let people know where they were going at all times. Such measures, although prudent, always annoyed her. They needed the killer behind bars so that the girls could walk around freely, not be scared for their lives while they were just going about their day.

The young, fresh faces of Roxie, Vicky, and Rose flashed before her, pinned up on the board in the task force room, their smiles a direct contrast to the frightened expression that she had just seen on Marla's face.

You will catch him, won't you?

She knocked on the door of the Student Services office, surprised when it was opened by a young guy who looked more like one of the students. She would have assumed that's exactly what he was if it wasn't for the staff badge on his lapel.

"Special Agent Price, FBI," she said. He looked at her, blinking rapidly, then opened the door and ushered her in. There was only one other person in the room, an older woman with frizzy hair who was furiously typing at a desk and didn't pause even when she looked up and nodded at Sadie.

"This is about those missing girls?" the young man asked, his right eye twitching. He seemed awkward, and even slightly hostile.

"They're no longer missing," Sadie told him, watching his right eye flicker more rapidly as she spoke. "You must have heard that Vicky Sable's body was found at the wharf the other morning? Well, I'm afraid we found Rose Perez in similar circumstances last night."

"It's been on the radio already," the frizzy-haired woman said without looking up from her computer. "But Guy here was in a meeting." She sounded slightly bitter, and Sadie realized that Guy must be her superior in the office. Given that he looked barely old enough to shave Sadie could understand why she was annoyed.

Perhaps Detective Linden felt similarly about her.

"Do you remember a student named Roxanne Miles, known as Roxie? She was killed in similar circumstances last year."

Guy went very still, and even the woman finally stopped typing and swiveled around in her chair to gape at Sadie. "You're saying it was the same guy?"

"We're examining that angle," Sadie said, not wanting to reveal too much before the chief held his official local press conference later that day. What with the murders and Westwood's arrest for abduction and rape, the local media would be all over him.

"Wasn't Roxie wrapped in plastic? Are you saying those other poor girls were killed the same way?" the woman asked, looking suitably horrified but also eager to hear more of the juicy details. Sadie suppressed a sigh. She never understood some people's fascination with true crime, as though reality was nothing but a soap opera.

"I'm not here to answer questions about the details of the case," Sadie said, her voice sharp. "I'm investigating. The killer is still running around out there."

The woman gave an exaggerated shudder, clearly not taking in Sadie's jibe.

"Well, I have access to all the student files right here," she said, patting her computer proudly. "So, anything you need to know…"

"Moira," Guy said, sounding angry, "I'll take this from here, you go and have an early break." It sounded like a demand rather than an offer and Moira glowered mutinously before standing up, shrugging on a coat, and stomping out of the office.

Sadie looked at Guy. His right eye had stopped twitching, but she hadn't been imagining the hostility. When he spoke his voice was frosty, and he sounded a lot older than he looked.

"So, what is it you need to know, Agent? Regardless of what Moira says, we keep only basic information on the students. The college counselors are the ones who would know anything deeply personal, or possibly their teachers."

"We'll get to them," Sadie assured him. "Local police are around campus too. We won't be leaving any stone unturned."

Guy's eye twitched uncontrollably. Was he just nervous, she wondered, or was that a guilty conscience? A sign that he was about to lie through his teeth?

"When students want to drop out of their courses," Sadie began, "it would be here they come, right?"

"Yes, certainly to finalize details," Guy said. "But in terms of discussing their feelings and options, they would be more likely to deal with the teachers or counselors, as I said."

"But you can look on that computer and tell me if a student either has or was about to drop out or not?"

Guy hesitated, then sighed and sat down at the desk Moira had vacated. "I do have a lot to do this morning," he muttered, as though Sadie's request was an unforgivable intrusion on his time.

"And I have a murderer to catch," Sadie snapped, losing her patience. Her nerves felt frayed, and she couldn't shake the feeling that this case was a ticking time bomb. That if this guy could kill two women in two days, then there was a third on the horizon.

And she was running out of time.

"Yes, Roxie dropped out," Guy told her after a few minutes of clicking through files. "She was killed the day before she was due to leave campus. And Victoria Sable had requested to defer for a year. So she might have been coming back, but they rarely do."

"And Rose Perez?" Sadie asked, holding her breath. She stood behind Guy, watching the screen, and read the notes for herself even as he relayed the information that she had requested.

"There's no record of any request being put in, no," he said. "She hasn't applied to speak to either the Careers Counselor or the mental health support team, either."

"But she was behind in her studies, right?" Sadie asked, leaning over his shoulder to make sure Guy wasn't leaving anything out.

"We wouldn't know that unless there's been action taken regarding her dropping out, deferring, or applying for retakes. You would need to speak to her instructors."

Sadie nodded. "Okay. You have to access to their schedules though, right?"

Guy looked twitchy again, and Sadie wondered if he just resented being asked to actually do any work, or if she should be considering him as a suspect. He certainly had plenty of access to and information about the victims.

"You want me to find you all of her classes?"

"Yes. I need her schedule, who her teachers and mentors are. And the same for Victoria and Roxanne."

Guy muttered under his breath but got on with her request, locating and printing off the files that she had asked for. Sadie took them with a murmured thanks and then scanned the pages, flicking through and back again, looking for any similarities. One name stood out.

"They all had the same instructor for Social Policy and Sports Science," she said, almost to herself.

"Yes, Ms. Dickens. She teaches both."

"Where is she now?" Sadie asked.

Sighing again, Guy turned back to the computer to look at the class schedules. His next words sent a prickle down Sadie's spine.

"It's her week off. She's had it booked for a while."

Sadie told herself it was too far out a theory, but it wouldn't be the first time that investigators had been stumped by assuming they were looking for a man when the perpetrator was actually a woman. Female serial killers were incredibly rare, but they happened. Most often as part of a male and female duo. A female acting alone was even rarer.

But it was possible, and it would explain the seeming lack of a sexual motive, which was odd in a case like this. Anyone could pose as "Brett" online, and it didn't take much typically male upper body strength to inject someone, stab them, and wrap them up. Although it would, admittedly, take a lot more strength to move them around, especially to get them up to the rafters of the warehouse. Which made the possibility of a duo more likely.

Sadie shook her head to clear it. Just because the only person who had so far been proven to be a link between all three girls was Ms. Dickens, it didn't make her the killer. Neither did the possibly completely coincidental fact that she wasn't on campus.

But it certainly made her a person of interest.

"Can I get a phone number and address for her, please?"

Guy complied with her request and then stood up, clearly waiting for her to leave. Sadie smiled at him. "And you, Guy, have you got an alibi for yesterday and two nights ago?"

She watched the corner of his right eye do the rumba. "I… I was here yesterday. At work. With Moira."

"And two nights ago?"

"At home with my girlfriend. You can corroborate that."

"I will," Sadie assured him, then left the office with Guy practically running to shut the door behind her.

Sadie paused in the corridor, trying to absorb everything that she had just learned. She needed to take the information on the teacher back to Linden and go and speak to the woman. But she also needed to find out about Detective Boyd, and she couldn't help wondering how Linden would react to that. But whether the detective liked it or not, Marla's information put Detective Boyd under suspicion. If it was something innocent and easily explainable, why hadn't Boyd mentioned it on the way to the campus, even if in passing?

Sadie was about to walk off down the corridor when she saw the sign on the door opposite.

Campus Security.

The department that Boyd would have been working for during his stint on campus.

Taking a deep breath, Sadie walked across the corridor and knocked on the door.

CHAPTER TWENTY ONE

The man who answered the door was somewhere between Linden's and Boyd's age, with graying temples and hazel eyes. He smiled at Sadie politely, then his smile vanished as he saw her badge.

"Come in," he said, his face serious now. He at least seemed a lot more willing to speak to her than Guy had been. He shut the door behind her and ran a hand through curly dark brown hair in a gesture that reminded her of Cooper.

She wished the sheriff was here to bounce ideas off. She missed working with him.

"I've just spoken to the APD," he told her. "Some guy called Detective Styles?"

Sadie nodded.

"So I'm not sure that I can tell you anything I didn't tell him," he said apologetically. "There have been no suspicious incidents on campus, no major issues with students. Thank God, we haven't been affected by this wave of sexual assault allegations on campus colleges—not yet anyway. I'm not so naïve as to think it never goes on here. But I don't really have any information to give you."

"Did you know the victims?"

The security chief—Teddy, according to his badge—shook his head. "I vaguely recognized the pictures, but to be honest, the students start to look the same after a while. I have more interactions with the guys—things getting out of hand at frat parties and things like that."

"I'm actually here to ask you about something else," Sadie said. "I believe a Kirk Boyd worked here last year, briefly, as security?"

"Yeah," Teddy said, his face brightening. "He was good to have around, he's a funny guy. Hang on." His eyes widened. "He isn't hurt, is he?"

"He's absolutely fine, or at least he was an hour or so ago," Sadie assured him. She wondered what the security chief would make of Marla's allegations. "I have a few questions about his conduct while he was here. Was he ever in trouble? Any complaints against him or anything like that?"

The security chief looked taken aback, but then his eyes narrowed suspiciously. "He's being hounded again, and by the FBI now. You guys are a piece of work. You must know he was cleared?"

"Cleared?" Sadie shook her head to indicate that she had no idea what Teddy was talking about, but he crossed his arms in front of his chest, clearly not believing a word of it.

"Well, it's not a secret, but I guess you guys don't talk to local cops much. Kirk—Detective Boyd—was working here while he was suspended from the Anchorage Police Department pending investigation. Just doing a bit of moonlighting, you know, to keep his mind off things. It was horrible, the way they just turfed him out and then once he was cleared, expected him to come back without even an apology. Of course, he did, he loves his job."

Sadie felt the prickling along her spine again and exhaled slightly. She had a suspicion that she knew exactly what Boyd had been suspended for.

"What were the allegations about?"

Teddy raised an eyebrow at her. "You don't know? Then why are you here?"

Sadie sighed. "I was interviewing a student earlier," she told him, deciding to come clean but making sure to protect Marla, "and I was with Detective Boyd. The student—a female—was obviously very uncomfortable. She spoke to me afterwards to tell me that Boyd had a reputation for being somewhat 'creepy' around the girls. Peering through their windows in the guise of checking on them. Given what's happened, it's important I check that out."

The security chief shook his head, looking nonplussed. "I don't understand why these things keep getting said about him," he said. "Look, I'm not saying Kirk's perfect—he's a big gambler, for one—but I've known him for years and he's no pervert. I actually had no problems with his performance here. If the allegations about him were true, do you think I would have employed him? He was cleared. It's not right for you to be bringing it up again now."

"You still haven't told me what the allegations were," Sadie pointed out, trying not to sound impatient. The security chief obviously considered "Kirk" to be a friend, and not wanting to believe the worst of people you knew was a phenomenon that Sadie came across often. Nobody ever wanted to believe that heinous crimes could be committed by the guy next door, or the guy they went hunting with, or the local teacher or pastor.

And especially not the local cop.

"He was accused of sexually assaulting some woman he arrested, that's about as much as I know," he told her. "And like I said, he was cleared."

"I hear that. But you're saying you didn't believe it even before he was cleared, otherwise you wouldn't have employed him?"

"That's right. Like I said, he's a decent guy. He was really upset about the suspension; he couldn't believe he had been accused of something like that. He's a good cop, most people around the city know him. I don't think anyone who knows him would have believed it."

"So as far as you know, there haven't been any previous allegations? And you had absolutely no concerns while he was here."

"Absolutely not," Teddy said, shaking his head resolutely. "How many times do you need me to tell you?" he challenged, and then sighed, holding his hands open apologetically. "Look, Agent, I'm sorry, but you're barking up the wrong tree here."

"Okay," Sadie said, seeing that she would get nowhere with him. He clearly believed in his friend and pushing him would just make it look as though she had an axe to grind. She would have to find out the details of Boyd's suspension back at the station—assuming that anyone would tell her. The thought of having to demand formal access to the files while in the middle of working on this with Detective Linden was a headache that none of them needed.

Surely, she thought, Linden would find this as suspicious as she did when he heard about Marla's statement. But she wouldn't put it past Linden to dismiss Marla as a hysterical female either.

There was only one way to find out.

She thanked the security chief and then left, making her way out of the building and toward her truck, ignoring the stares and whispers of the students as she went past. As she got back into her truck, she called O'Hara to fill him in.

Agent O'Hara sounded less than happy. "I'm just being ignored," he complained. "The local cops are so convinced we're going to take over the case that they seem determined to not let me speak at all."

Sadie sympathized with him, but she also knew that O'Hara needed to learn to assert himself. He was still a new agent in the first year of service, and it wouldn't be the last time he faced feeling sidelined.

"Did you get anything on the Jaguar?"

"The car owners checked out—no links to the case, both have a verifiable alibi. The car rental place is being hostile so we've applied for a formal warrant, so we should get that by later today. What about you?"

Sadie took a deep breath before she told him about both Ms. Dickens and Detective Boyd. O'Hara whistled quietly.

"I'm going to check out Ms. Dickens on the way back to the station," Sadie told him. "I'll meet you there."

Linden was convening the task force again after lunch, but Sadie wanted to do some digging on Boyd first; she could hardly announce him as a potential suspect while he was in the room.

As she drove, Sadie found herself replaying the conversation with O'Hara in her head, but this time it was Sheriff Cooper she was talking to. Her feelings for him aside, she worked well with Cooper. He was a logical thinker, if a little too cautious in Sadie's opinion, but also not afraid to challenge the status quo, and Sadie was missing his insight on what was turning out to be a baffling case. O'Hara was shaping up to be a good agent, but he wasn't Cooper.

She thought about phoning the sheriff to get his opinion, but something stopped her. Talking to Cooper meant bringing up the memories of everything he had told her the night before, and she couldn't afford to be distracted by that now. As much as part of her wanted to leave this case to Detective Linden and drive back to the cave to find out what the hell had happened to her family, the agent in her needed to solve this case. Needed to find justice for the victims.

Even if it meant taking down a cop.

CHAPTER TWENTY TWO

He watched the girl walking toward him across the small park, the cold noon sunlight glittering on her hair, which had escaped from its scarf and was flying in tendrils around her face. She had made an effort to look pretty, outlining her large eyes and mouth so they stood out against her pale face.

Like a fish, he thought with contempt. She had stopped walking now, staring around her aimlessly with those big, stupid eyes. Looking for him.

Or rather, not him, but Brett. They were such fools, believing everything some unknown face on the internet told them. Letting him reel them in like cod on a hook.

This part, the catch, was the best bet.

Or maybe, the second-best bit.

He had to stop himself from licking his lips as he watched her, enjoying her confusion and the look of disappointment as she started to wonder if she was being stood up. Now was the moment he needed to act, but it was also the most precarious moment, when she could wriggle away from his net.

He stood up and walked toward her, and she looked at him, startled, then puzzled. He saw her register recognition.

"Do I know you? You look familiar." She squinted at him, trying to figure out where she had seen his face before. He felt the blood pumping in his veins. He was so, so close to her. So close to the catch.

He had to be careful not to lose her at the last, precious moment. Or he would lose everything.

They were on to him now; he had to be careful. "Brett" had to die. The avatar had served his purpose and it was time to lie low for a while, until he could strike again. He had nearly cancelled this one, knowing that three catches in three days was pushing his luck, but once he had started reeling her in, he couldn't bring himself to stop. The thought of having her in his arms was all encompassing now.

He held the rose out to her from where he had been holding it behind his back.

"Surprise," he said, his voice soft and seductive. But she wasn't quite as polite as the others. She stepped back, a look of anger crossing her face.

"Where's Brett?" she asked. Her phone was in her hand, and he could see her about to lift it. To call for help.

He had to act now.

He lunged for her and had the needle in her neck before she could react. He put his arm around her, holding her up and walking briskly toward where his vehicle was hidden behind the trees, looking around him surreptitiously to make sure no one had seen. But the area was almost deserted. The late February weather was sharp enough that few people were visiting the small park, which was still buried under snow.

She sagged in his arms, trying to speak, her legs moving in the direction that he was propelling her, but too slowly. She would be fully unconscious within seconds, he knew.

She tried to speak again, her voice slurred and dribbling at the corners of her mouth, and he felt the usual disgust for them overtake him. Once they were passive and helpless, when he could do what he wanted with them, then he was interested, but not when they were like this, drooling and gibbering.

He bundled her into the car, his heart rate rising, feeling anger at her for forcing him to have to do this, for not complying as the others did. She was making him waste time and effort.

His temper cooled as he drove and she quieted down, slipping into content oblivion, so still now that she looked dead.

It wouldn't be long.

He would have to change his dumping ground this time. He had seen the cops swarming the wharf; they even had the FBI investigating. That gave him a buzz, knowing that he was deemed so important and that the world, finally, was taking notice of him. That they could look at the bodies of the girls and see what he had always known; that they were nothing, no more significant than the bodies you could buy at the fish market, with their staring eyes and stupid, lolling mouths. They were nothing. But he, he was somebody now, and even if they caught him, they could never take that away from him.

He didn't want to be caught though; not yet. Not while the urge to hunt was still so strong in him. It was going to be hard after this, to lie low and keep his head down.

Perhaps he should move and find a new hunting ground entirely. He couldn't keep using the college, not now that they were all prowling around, looking for him, having no idea that he was right under their noses.

He glanced at the young woman in the seat next to him and saw that her skin had gone waxy and pale. He checked for a pulse, panicking for a moment that he had given her too much and she was already dead, then breathed a large sigh of relief as his fears proved unfounded. He would need to hurry up though, he was sure. It had to be timed just right.

He liked them to be just conscious enough that they flinched when he gutted them, wriggling slightly as he wrapped them up. Packing their flesh.

He couldn't wait.

He licked his lips and hit the gas.

CHAPTER TWENTY THREE

Linden and the rest of the task force were already back at the station when Sadie arrived. She looked around for Detective Boyd, noting that there was no sign of him, and felt a flutter of panic. Where was he? Out hunting again already?

With Ms. Dickens having proven to be a dead end, Sadie was feeling more and more worried about Boyd. She was going to have to raise it with Linden and, if Boyd wasn't located fast, the rest of the task force. Sadie didn't care if Linden didn't agree; they had enough circumstantial evidence to make questioning Detective Boyd a priority.

She had driven to Ms. Dickens's house to find it locked up and no vehicle in the driveway. A chat with her sweet old neighbors had revealed that the teacher had gone on vacation for the week and that they were looking after her dog. Ms. Dickens, apparently, was approaching retirement age and used a walking stick. Although Sadie would make sure that someone corroborated that Ms. Dickens had indeed checked in to her planned resort, she was fairly confident that the teacher could be ruled out as a suspect.

It was strange, though, that Guy from Student Services hadn't mentioned it. Perhaps, like so many people, he hadn't realized the teacher could be viewed as a suspect simply because she was a woman.

O'Hara looked up as Sadie walked into the room. He was standing in the corner with a coffee, next to Linden and Styles, who were talking in low voices, their backs very obviously facing O'Hara as though ignoring the agent's presence.

Linden looked up as he saw Sadie approach.

"Where's Boyd?" he snapped. "And where did you go?"

Sadie motioned for him to come over. Looking annoyed, Linden sighed heavily but walked over to her, leaving Styles where he was.

"What is it, Price?" he said, and then continued before Sadie could respond. "I don't appreciate you going off and doing your own thing. We don't need mavericks on the task force."

"Rose Perez's roommate had something to tell me, and she wanted to disclose to me alone," Sadie said.

Linden's expression softened a little. "Like I said, women work best with other women," he said, as if this confirmed all of his sexist assumptions. Sadie bit down her retort. It could wait.

"Did you know Detective Boyd worked as security on campus while he was suspended from the police department?" she asked icily. The more she thought about it, the more annoyed she was that no one had thought it was worth mentioning, or that Linden had ever thought he was an appropriate person to investigate this case.

"What of it?" Linden snapped.

"There have been reports that while he was there, the female students found him 'creepy.' A few of them thought he was hanging around their bedrooms a bit too much at night. Peering through ground floor windows, that kind of thing."

Linden looked startled and glared at her. "Official reports?" he asked, his voice dripping with sudden sarcasm.

"No," Sadie admitted. "But—"

"And this was never mentioned at the time? Agent Price, this is probably just fearmongering. I'm sure the girls on campus are scared right now, and probably working themselves up. It sounds as though you're just repeating gossip to me."

"I'm a federal agent," Sadie said tightly. "I don't 'gossip.' You don't think that's just a bit too much of a coincidence? Especially when you consider what Detective Boyd was suspended for."

"Detective Boyd was cleared!" Linden roared suddenly, causing Styles and O'Hara to look over. O'Hara started walking toward them, concern etched on his face. "We all knew he was innocent. The complaint came from a woman with a rap sheet as long as your arm, who makes a complaint every time she is arrested. But of course, we had to follow protocol and conduct an investigation. There was clear CCTV evidence showing that Boyd didn't lay a hand on her while arresting her. He was completely cleared. Do you think I would have put him on this case if I had any indication that he was guilty? How dare you question my professional judgment!" He looked outraged, spittle flying from his face, and Sadie stepped back, surprised at his sudden outburst.

"I'm not questioning anyone's judgment," Sadie said calmly. "But given the reports about his behavior on campus, we need to be questioning him at the very least."

"I'm happy to do that with Sadie," O'Hara said from behind Linden, "if it's too uncomfortable for you, Detective."

As Linden whirled around to face O'Hara, Sadie thought he was going to start shouting again. Instead, he shook his head incredulously.

"Do you seriously think that Boyd could be Brett?" he said, laughing harshly, although he didn't look amused in the slightest. "Does he strike you as someone who uses Facebook? Or even knows how to?"

That was a fair point, Sadie conceded. "Even so, I wouldn't be doing my job properly if I didn't think it was worth questioning him. If he was peering through the girls' windows, he may have noticed something pertinent without even realizing it. And it seems odd that he came to campus with me and didn't once mention he had worked there."

"He probably guessed that you would suspect him," Linden huffed. "Perhaps you need to go home and get some sleep, Agent. The long hours seem to be addling your brain."

Sadie had had enough of his jibes. She was about to retort when O'Hara cut in quickly. "Well, where is he? If he was here then we could just ask him, couldn't we?"

Sadie nodded. "You're complaining about me going off on my own," she pointed out to Linden, "yet you don't know where your usual partner is?"

Linden looked angry but of course could hardly argue with Sadie's comment. He pulled his phone out of his pocket and stomped off, presumably to track down Detective Boyd. O'Hara raised his eyebrows at Linden's departing back. "Well, that didn't go down very well," he said.

"Understatement of the century," Sadie murmured. She looked over at the board, and something caught her attention. New locations had been added to the map which plotted the campus dorms, the wharf, and the bus station. Westwood's mansion, she noticed, was also still on there. Seeing her looking, Styles came over, looking awkward.

"Er, sorry about Detective Linden," he said. "He doesn't like being challenged."

"I've noticed," Sadie said. Styles laughed awkwardly, then motioned to the board that she had been looking at.

"I heard what you were saying about Detective Boyd," he said, "and I don't have an opinion on him. I don't work with him very often. But I've been adding locations to the map that the killer could be using or could use in the future. We can't see him risking the wharf again, right? And we know he's a fisherman or at least around the fishing industry."

Sadie nodded. "Good idea," she said, scanning the board. "So, what has that got to do with Boyd?"

Styles swallowed, looking uncomfortable. "Well, I added this spot here, where there are a few fishing cabins on the pier. It's out of the way and not used often, so I thought it could be worth checking out. He can't be gutting and wrapping up girls anywhere near a busy fishing port, can he? But when I added it, Boyd seemed…I don't know, a bit agitated. He owns one of them, I think. I was about to ask him if he knew much about who owned the other cabins, but he cut me off. Then he headed off. I assumed he was catching up with you, but obviously not. I don't want to think Boyd has anything to do with this, but he might know something."

Sadie was about to reply, to ask Styles exactly what he meant by Boyd being 'agitated,' when her phone rang. It was Marla again. Moving away to get some privacy, she answered it.

"Hello, Marla? Is everything okay?"

"Agent Price. Hi. Um, I don't want to bother you, but you said if there was anything…" Marla sounded uncertain and her voice was low, as though she didn't want to be overhead. Judging by the sound of chatter and clinking dishes in the background, she was in the college cafeteria.

"It's just…one of my classmates didn't turn up for the lecture this morning, and her roommates say she didn't tell them she was skipping, but she got up and went out early. I know it's probably nothing, I can't report her missing or anything, but I just thought you should know. Just in case…" Marla left the sentence unfinished, but they both knew exactly what she meant.

Sadie felt a sense of dread curling in the pit of her stomach, a gut instinct that told her that, no matter how much common sense may dictate that a college kid skipping class was nothing to worry about, she should in fact be very worried indeed.

"What's her name, Marla?"

"Annie Tyler. I don't know her very well. I'm sorry, I'm probably wasting your time…"

"No," Sadie cut in sharply. "You're not at all. If there's anything else you can tell me, even if you think it's irrelevant, please do. Can you check if she's in her afternoon classes?"

"Er, yeah. She should be in History with my friend. I'll let you know."

"Thank you, Marla," Sadie said briskly. She was trying not to sound concerned, to not start a panic on campus unnecessarily. But as soon as she ended the call she looked from Agent O'Hara to Styles and felt the horror filling her eyes.

"Sadie, what is it?" O'Hara was already reaching for his jacket.

"That was Marla," she said, trying to keep her voice steady. "One of her classmates hasn't turned up for class, a young woman named Annie Tyler."

Styles looked puzzled. "Is there any reason to think she's in danger? I mean, skipping class is pretty common, right?"

"I know," said Sadie. "But I want to check it out anyway. Let Detective Linden know, Styles. I'll take Agent O'Hara with me."

"You're going back to campus?" Styles assumed.

"No," Sadie said, shaking her head and looking at the board in front of her. "I'm going to check out those fishing cabins."

She ignored Styles's look of bewilderment and left the room, almost running. O'Hara kept up with her with his long, gangly strides.

"Don't you want to alert Linden?"

"No, Styles can tell him," Sadie said shortly. "I've got no doubt that he will think I'm overreacting, and you can see what he thought of my asking questions about Detective Boyd. And if I am wrong, which I may well be, then the fewer of us off on a wild goose chase, the better."

O'Hara nodded, and Sadie thought how refreshing it was that he seemed to completely trust her hunch. Even Cooper would be arguing with her right now, although he had plenty of experience of Sadie's intuition being startlingly accurate.

It wasn't a trait about herself that Sadie necessarily saw as an advantage, at least on a personal level. For while her intuition had helped her solve many a difficult case, it had also gotten her into a lot of trouble, something else that Sheriff Cooper would attest to. In fact, having worked with him for a few months now, she was often at a loss to understand exactly what it was that he liked about her.

They climbed into her truck and Sadie had pulled off before O'Hara had even finished belting himself in.

"You really think this girl might be danger?" he said, his face pale.

Sadie nodded. "If you look at the timeframe between Vicky and Rose, then yeah. If this guy is off on some kind of killing spree, then we are about due another body."

O'Hara looked unconvinced. "But isn't it risky, three victims so close to each other?"

"Yes," Sadie agreed. "But so was two. I think he's past the point of thinking rationally in any way. He's taking his chances on getting caught; maybe he's even determined to kill as many victims as possible before he does, or maybe he's too disconnected from reality to care. Who knows? But until we know different, I think we should assume this spree is going to continue along similar lines."

"Unless we stop him," O'Hara said grimly.

"Right. And I'm not waiting for Linden to get his head out of his ass. Quite frankly, O'Hara, I'll take my chances of being wrong and looking like a hothead than of being right and leaving it too late."

O'Hara looked at her in admiration, but Sadie barely registered it. Her thoughts were on Detective Boyd, Annie Tyler, and those out of the way fishing cabins.

Where fishermen caught and gutted their catch.

Not for the first time, Sadie really, really hoped that her hunch was wrong.

Because if she was right, then Annie Tyler was in serious danger.

And they were running out of time to save her.

CHAPTER TWENTY FOUR

Sadie drove out of Anchorage and along the coastal road, very quickly leaving civilization behind and driving into the more remote outreaches of the city, punctuated only by the odd fishing tackle shop and cabin. She could see the small piers with the private cabins in the distance and kept her eyes on the farthest one, her hands clammy on the wheel.

It was afternoon now and they only had a few hours of light left before it would rapidly grow dim and then dark. Arriving back in Alaska at the height of winter, Sadie had taken some time to adjust to the near perpetual darkness after the more temperate climate of Washington, DC. Now, she remembered Detective Boyd's comments about the dark and shuddered as she wondered if it had been himself that he had been referring to. If the long winter had set off his killing instinct.

Sadie shuddered at her own morbid thoughts, willing the long road to come to an end. Still hoping that she was wrong, and that Marla would call her any moment with the information that Annie Tyler was safe and well in her afternoon class.

Finally, they reached the first cabin. "Look!" O'Hara exclaimed, pointing to the vehicle parked outside, but Sadie had already spotted it as she took a sharp turn toward the cabin.

It was a sleek Jaguar sports car.

"Rental car, I bet," O'Hara muttered bitterly.

Sadie pulled up and got out. Her hand was on her gun, but she didn't pull it.

"Let's not go in like we're making arrests," Sadie warned him. Or maybe she was warning herself. With the Mangler case about to come to a decision, she didn't need any further accusations of being trigger happy.

At the same time, she wasn't about to hold back if someone's life was in danger.

They approached the door of the cabin quietly. It was one of the newer ones, not like some of the more ramshackle affairs often seen at this end of town. Judging by the car and the pristine state of the cabin, whoever fished here had some money, and obviously used the cabin a lot to take such good care of it. She had known they were looking for a fisherman, but somehow this wasn't quite what she had expected.

Sadie knocked on the door, her hand still on her holster. O'Hara hovered close behind her, and she could sense the tension in his own body. Sadie realized that she was holding her breath.

A few minutes later she let it out in frustration as it became apparent that no one was about to answer the door.

"There must be someone about, if the vehicle's here," O'Hara grumbled.

"Could be out on his boat," Sadie said. "Let's go take a look."

They were about to walk around to the back of the cabin—or front of the pier—when they heard footsteps coming the other way, and a voice whistling cheerfully.

A man appeared around the side of the cabin, looking surprised as the whistling died in his throat, carrying a fishing rod and tackle box.

"Agent Price?"

It wasn't Detective Boyd.

It was Teddy, the security chief from the college campus. He looked from her to O'Hara, seeming genuinely puzzled.

"Can I help you?"

"Is that your vehicle, sir?" O'Hara asked. His tone was polite, but the edge in his voice was obvious. Sadie could feel the pulse working in her throat as she scanned Teddy.

"Yes, it is. Well, it's a rental, actually. Mine's been in the garage, getting the turbo changed. It's costing me a fortune, I can tell you that much."

"We were looking for Detective Boyd," Sadie said.

Teddy frowned. "Shouldn't he be at the station with you guys? He does fish with me here a lot—he owns the next cabin down—but not today. I wasn't actually planning on it myself, not straight after coming off shift at the college, but I needed some downtime. You know, with everything going on." He shrugged.

"Of course," Sadie replied, forcing herself to be polite even while the hairs on the back of her neck were standing on end. "Would you mind if we came in and had a look around?"

"No, of course not, come in." The security chief seemed unperturbed as he let them in to the cabin.

Too much so, Sadie thought. Who wasn't nervous when the FBI turned up on their doorstep after two of the students on their watch had been brutally murdered? He was acting, and he was very good at it. O'Hara seemed to have relaxed somewhat, as though he was half falling for Teddy's charm.

The inside of the cabin was as smart as its outer appearance, with a small kitchenette and some cute nautical décor. It stunk of the sea, and of fish, of course, and she could hear the roar of the ocean through the back door that would lead down to the stoop.

"What is it you need to see? Shall I make some coffee?" Teddy started to fill the coffee machine as Sadie and O'Hara poked around, looking through his tackle and the adjoining room, which had a seating area and a stack of fishing books. There was no sign of anything untoward. As they went back into the kitchen, Teddy was placing cups of coffee on the table. Sadie lifted hers and held it without putting it to her mouth, but she saw that O'Hara was already sipping his.

"Could we have a look on your boat, too, Teddy?"

The security chief raised an eyebrow. "You're not going to find Detective Boyd on there, Agent Price," he laughed, and then said more seriously, "I can promise you, I'm not hiding him from you. Boyd borrows my car sometimes, but not my boat."

"Even so," Sadie said tightly, alarm signals going off in her mind. Were they working together? Or was Teddy just covering his tracks, considering they'd already seen the Jaguar outside?

Or perhaps he really had nothing to do with any of it and Detective Boyd was a lot smarter than Sadie would have given him credit for.

"Okay, sure." He sounded reluctant but made his way to the back door and headed out onto the stoop. Sadie and O'Hara followed him down to the boat, hanging a little way behind.

Down on the water's edge, a path led around the coast, disappearing into a thicket of shrubby trees. Sadie looked across at them, seeing a corrugated tin roof just visible through the branches.

"I think he's clean," O'Hara whispered as they watched Teddy pulling the tarpaulin back from the boat. "We should check out Boyd's cabin. He already said that Boyd has borrowed his car."

"Let's see the boat first," Sadie murmured back, watching Teddy carefully in case he was about to pull a weapon on them. Instead, he stepped aboard and motioned for them to follow. As he showed them around the boat, he seemed incredibly proud of it, as most fishermen were of their boats. Everything seemed so normal that Sadie started to wonder if O'Hara was right, and they were just wasting time on Teddy.

Wasting time while Annie Tyler was dying somewhere.

There was nothing on the boat, and they followed Teddy back around the cabin as he chattered inanely to O'Hara about fishing and boats in general. Sadie hung back, scanning the roof that she could see along the coastal path.

"What's that building?" she asked, pointing to it.

Teddy looked back at her and followed the direction of her raised arm.

And she saw him flinch. Saw the sudden, blink-and-you-miss-it micro-expression of guilt that crossed his face before it went back to the friendly, slightly puzzled expression that he had been wearing since they had arrived.

"Oh, just some old outhouse," he said. "No one uses it."

"It doesn't belong to any of the cabins?"

"Not that I know of," he said. Again, too casually. Sadie just nodded and continued walking, but she felt Teddy's eyes linger on her just a little too long.

As they reached the front of the cabin, Teddy smiled at them before going back inside. "If I see Boyd, is there anything I should tell him?"

"Just to get in touch with myself or Detective Linden," Sadie said stiffly. She watched Teddy go inside and then turned to O'Hara. "You believe him?"

O'Hara shrugged. "Maybe. I think we need to get to Boyd's cabin."

Sadie shook her head. "I saw his reaction when I asked him about the outhouse. I want to check that out first."

O'Hara frowned but shrugged in acquiescence.

"We can split up," Sadie said. "It will save time. You go see if Boyd is at his cabin and I'll check out the outhouse. Make sure your radio is on hand."

O'Hara still looked uncertain. He also, Sadie thought, looked slightly waxy, as though he was nauseous. "Sadie, the last case we worked, when you went off alone, you nearly died…" He trailed off, clutching his stomach.

"O'Hara? What is it?" Sadie asked as O'Hara slumped against the side of the truck, his eyelids fluttering.

"I feel…weird…" he mumbled, his words slurring. Was he having some kind of seizure? Then it hit Sadie that she knew exactly what was wrong.

The coffee.

As O'Hara slumped to the ground and Sadie leaned over to grab him, she heard the cabin door open and saw Teddy rushing at her out of the side of her vision. She immediately grabbed her gun, twisting painfully to both draw it and try to shield O'Hara, but Teddy was already on her, knocking her forcefully back against the truck even as she heard him cock a shotgun.

Caught off guard and also off balance, Sadie banged painfully into the truck, feeling the breath leave her body, winding her. Her gun went skittering across the hood of the truck, and she heard it land somewhere on the other side.

Trying to ignore the searing pain in her gut, Sadie kicked out at Teddy. Her foot landed squarely in his thigh and although he went stumbling backwards, he didn't let go of his gun. He raised it and fired wildly, just as Sadie threw herself to the ground and rolled swiftly under the truck, looking out the other side for her gun.

At first, she couldn't see it, but then she spotted it a few feet across the drive, lying near a bush. She pulled herself forward on her forearms, commando crawling, and made a break for it out of the other side of the truck, running at a crouch toward her pistol.

"Stop right there or I'll kill him."

For a split second Sadie would have continued toward her gun, just a couple of feet away, but there was a steely certainty in Teddy's voice that struck her immediately. He meant every word he said. Sadie straightened slowly and looked over her shoulder, still poised to make a dash for it.

Teddy had dragged an unconscious O'Hara around the side of the truck and was lifting his head up by his hair. Teddy's shotgun was jammed into O'Hara's temple, and the security chief's eyes glittered dangerously.

"Put your hands in the air and turn around," Teddy said, almost mockingly, as though he was the law enforcement officer and she was the criminal. Biting back her anger, Sadie did as she was told, her hands raised as she pivoted slowly on her heels. Her body was still tense, ready to make a break for it at the first opportune moment, but right now hers and O'Hara's prospects were not looking good.

O'Hara's skin looked waxy, and she couldn't see the rise and fall of his chest.

"Let me call an ambulance for him," she said, trying to sound reasonable to deescalate Teddy. As though they were just having a pleasant chit-chat on his driveway. "Whatever you've given him, you've given him too much. Call him an ambulance, and I'll come inside with you. We can talk."

Teddy just laughed, but it was a hollow sound, devoid of humor, and the glint in his eyes now was one of hatred.

"Do you really think you're in any position to bargain with me, Agent? I'll be giving the orders around here from now on. And your friend here is going to die one way or the other. Better it's a peaceful death, eh?"

Sadie didn't reply. She knew when she was trapped.

Keeping the butt of his gun firmly in Agent O'Hara's temple, Teddy reached into his pocket, pulled out a pair of handcuffs, and tossed them to Sadie, who caught them in one of her outstretched hands.

"Put them on," he told her.

Sadie didn't move. Her mouth was dry, and her tongue felt like a thick wad of sandpaper. She glared at Teddy as he gave her a malicious smile.

"Do it, Agent Price," he said, "or I'll kill him and then you where you stand."

"We're on an open driveway," she said. "You'll be seen."

Teddy laughed. "By who? You see anyone around here, Agent? The cabin next to me is owned by Boyd, and the one next to him is only used in the summer. No one drives along this way. It's just you and me." He smiled at his last words, his voice dropping in a mockery of intimacy that made her skin crawl.

"Where is Detective Boyd?" Sadie asked, still trying to stall for time. Teddy smiled again. Sadie was aching to wipe that smile off his face, if she ever got the chance.

But it wasn't looking very likely.

In fact, right now, it wasn't looking likely that she was getting out of here alive.

CHAPTER TWENTY FIVE

"You don't really have any choice," Teddy said to her, almost conversationally. In that moment, Sadie didn't think she had ever hated anybody quite so much. How had she not noticed this level of malevolence when she had first questioned him? Usually, Sadie was fairly good at assessing people's characters, but Teddy's hidden side had been, on that first encounter, very well hidden indeed.

But that was hardly unusual with serial killers. Her thoughts flashed back to the Boston Mangler, who had been a quiet, unassuming man, whom no one had unsuspected until Sadie, and that had been nearly too late. She had been lucky to survive that one.

Only to end up here, with an equally psychopathic maniac pointing a shotgun at her junior partner while smirking at her as though this was all a joke. She wanted to strangle him with her bare hands, and her fingers curled reflexively around the cuffs that she was now holding.

"That's right, Agent," he told her. "Put the cuffs on, with your hands in front of you, and then we'll leave your friend here to have a little sleep while me and you go for a walk, eh?"

"I'm not going anywhere with you," Sadie snapped, but she knew it was bravado. Playing for time, in the hopes that one of the task force had decided to follow her out here. Sadie preferred to save herself, but beggars couldn't be choosers and right now some timely intervention would be more than welcome.

But she knew it wouldn't happen. Linden no doubt thought she was off on a wild goose chase and would leave her to it.

Unless Detective Boyd didn't turn up.

Unless Annie Tyler was reported missing.

"Where's Boyd?" Sadie asked Teddy.

"I'm taking you to him. He's going to be thrilled to see you."

Sadie felt her stomach roil with nausea at the thought of Teddy and Boyd working together. Gutting her. Wrapping her up in plastic and leaving her to bleed out in the nearby wharf.

Something in Teddy's voice gave that thought pause though. If he was working with Boyd, then why wasn't the detective here?

Perhaps because he's already at work on Annie Tyler, she thought, and had to stop herself from retching. Her stomach was still in knots from where Teddy had winded her, and her right side felt cut and grazed from where she had thrown herself under the truck. But she was only dimly aware of the painful sensations in her body as she stared Teddy down, still hoping for a way out. Because if she ended up with the cuffs on, then escaping was going to be a hell of a lot harder.

And she *had* to escape. The alternatives were unthinkable.

"Handcuffs, Agent Price," Teddy said. "I'm starting to get bored. If you don't hurry up, I might kill your boyfriend here just for fun." He rammed his gun harder into O'Hara's head.

Sadie wondered if she should just chance it and run for her gun and hope Teddy's bullet wouldn't hit her in time. Because O'Hara looked already dead, and if he was then she was sacrificing herself for nothing.

But what if he was alive? Sadie knew she would never forgive herself. And the chances were too slim. If she turned and dived for her gun now, it was still far enough away that Teddy would have plenty of time to shoot O'Hara and then her, straight in the back.

Teddy was right. She had no choice.

Keeping her face blank and refusing to show her fear, Sadie clicked on the cuffs. Teddy gave her a wide grin that made her blood boil even more.

"Good girl. Now start walking around the cabin towards the stoop. I'll be right behind you."

Sadie did as she was told, her legs moving as though through molasses. She moved as slowly as possible, still stalling as much as she could in the hopes that some kind of plan or opportunity would present itself, until she felt Teddy's shotgun in her back, pushing her sharply forward.

"Move!" He barked the word, and she could hear fury in his voice now. "Keep messing me around, Agent, and I will just kill you here. You're starting to become less fun than I thought you would be."

They walked past the cabin and down toward the stoop. The icy ocean was calm today, the late afternoon sun glittering on it, a deep golden yellow that would turn to sunset in less than an hour. Teddy's boat bobbed up and down, looking all too ordinary, a picture postcard scene, and Sadie felt a sudden and intense aching for the beauties of life.

Knowing you were about to die did that to a girl.

She was expecting him to take her onto the boat, but at the last minute he told her to turn right, along the coastal path. Although "path" was a generous word for the slippery, icy track that ran past the scrubby woods and on to the next stoop.

The one that belonged to Detective Boyd.

That must be where he was taking her. To Boyd's cabin. Would she find Annie Tyler there, and if so, was the girl still alive, or already dead?

She tried not to think of Linden's face when he found not just one more victim, but two, and one of them Sadie herself. It would certainly prove him right about female agents, she thought with a sudden urge to laugh.

Then she thought about Cooper getting the news and wondered how he would take it. Would he cry? She couldn't imagine the big, handsome sheriff crying and yet she knew that Cooper had a vulnerable side.

It was one of the things she loved about him.

A gull cried, jerking her out of her thoughts, and she looked out over the ocean again, then stumbled on a patch of ice as Teddy roughly shoved her again with his gun.

"This isn't an afternoon stroll, Agent," he snapped. "Hurry up."

"You'll get caught, you know," Sadie said to him, almost casually, walking as slowly as she could without him shoving her again. "You've gone a bit too far now, don't you think? How are you going to get rid of three bodies?"

"Three?" Teddy said sharply.

"Annie Tyler," Sadie said, and then gasped as he grabbed her upper arm, twisting it back fiercely and with such force that, constrained as she was by the cuffs at the front, she was sure her arm would break. He was right up against her, with the gun wedged between them, and when he spoke she could hear his breath on her ear and the back of her neck.

"How do you know about her? She can't have been reported missing yet."

When Sadie didn't answer, knowing that the more unsettled he was the better chance of getting him off guard—assuming he didn't just panic and kill her—he yanked her arm again, causing a pain so crippling that she had to bite back a scream and her legs buckled beneath her. He dragged her back to her feet.

"She wasn't in class this morning," Sadie panted through the pain, breathing a sigh of relief when he relaxed his grip on her arm. Not much, but enough that it didn't feel as though it was about to break.

"And how do you know that?"

"There have just been two murders on campus," Sadie said, trying to sound reasonable. "Obviously, we're keeping an eye on things. You said yourself this morning you and your colleagues were all being questioned."

Teddy chuckled to himself, seemingly mollified by her answer. "You didn't have a clue either, did you? Any of you. You all spoke to me and believed every word I said."

Sadie nodded, knowing that playing to his ego was probably her best strategy right now, even if it rankled her. "You're right. You've been too clever for us."

He let go of her arm and shoved her with the gun again in the small of her back, as though she could possibly forget that it was there.

"Keep moving," he said, and Sadie started walking again. Her arm was throbbing. It was sprained, she thought, but not broken.

"So how did you do it?" she asked, trying to inject a note of curiosity, almost admiration, into her voice. "Detective Boyd identify potential targets, snooping around windows, and you lured them in online? There's no way he was smart enough to be Brett."

Teddy laughed, but he sounded annoyed, as though she had struck a wrong note with her attempted flattery. "You still think Boyd has anything to do with this?"

"He doesn't?" Sadie had the sudden image of Boyd back at the station, chatting with Linden about her mistakenly suspecting him, still none the wiser as to what was really going on.

"No," Teddy said sharply. "You think I needed his help?"

"No," Sadie said. "I assumed you were the brains of the operation. But I thought Detective Boyd was helping. We did have him in the frame after the complaints from the students, but I should have known he would never be able to pull something like this off. This takes intelligence."

"That's right," Teddy said smugly. That was one thing you could always rely on with psychopaths, Sadie thought wryly. Narcissistic and ego-driven to a fault.

"And Annie?" Sadie held her breath, waiting for him to grab her again, but he only continued marching her forward, then suddenly jerked her around, pushing her off the path and toward the patch of woodland.

"You're about to find out," he said, as Sadie saw the outhouse she had spotted earlier taking shape through the trees. It looked like a refurbished barn of some kind, and the windows, although clean on the outside, were blacked out from within.

This is where he's gutting them, Sadie thought with a stab of sheer terror.

Refusing to simply be led to her death, Sadie suddenly slumped downward as though she had fainted.

"What the hell?" Teddy reached down for her, and she felt the pressure of the shotgun ease off her back. Quick as lightning, Sadie rolled and kicked out, trying to ignore the pain in her ribs as she did so, feeling her boots connect with Teddy's legs. He stumbled off sideways, letting out a shot that mercifully went wide. She kicked again, aiming for the shotgun in his arms, but couldn't get enough height with her hands compromised and instead landed face down in the dirt.

"You little bitch!" Teddy roared behind her, lumbering toward her. Sadie pushed herself up on her hands and knees and jumped to her feet, running for the denser part of the trees. She would rather be shot in the back than walk willingly into Teddy's death pit.

But she didn't have enough of a head start, and even as Teddy closed the gap between them, she knew he was going to catch up with her. For a moment, she wondered why he didn't just shoot her, but then remembered that he would want her alive.

For now.

So she could end up gutted like Roxie, Victoria, and Rose.

And Annie?

Sadie roared with sudden rage and whirled around on her feet, clamping her hands together and aiming for Teddy's face. She wasn't going down without a fight. Not like this.

Then she saw him swinging the shotgun at her head and felt its full weight hit her, sending colorful sparks flying in front of her eyes as she slumped down to the ground, for real this time.

She tasted dirt again and coughed, trying to push herself up but unable to coordinate her arms and legs as her head throbbed with intense pain. As though from far away she was aware of him kicking her and cursing her loudly.

Then he hit her in the head with the shotgun again.

And Sadie's whole world went black.

CHAPTER TWENTY SIX

Sadie blinked against the half-light that met her eyes as she opened them, wincing at the sudden, sharp pain in her head. It took her a few moments to remember where she was, and who with, then she sat up sharply, nearly blacking out again as a white-hot pain exploded at her temples. She retched, but her stomach was too empty to release anything.

Then she retched again as the smell of fish hit her.

"Easy, Agent," a man chuckled across the room. Her vision was blurry, but she forced herself to look at him and Teddy swam into focus, smiling casually at her. He was sitting on an upturned barrel at the other side of the outhouse, and she had been dragged into the far corner. Her ankles were now shackled as well as her wrists. His shotgun was in his lap, but it was trained on her and his finger was resting lightly on the trigger. She took a deep breath, trying not to heave again at the smell of brine, and looked around her.

Buckets full of fish lay just feet from her, explaining the smell. But it wasn't the smell that made her want to vomit.

A giant plastic sheet dispenser lay along the back wall, and in front of it was a surgical table, with a naked woman shackled down to it. Her head lolled to the side, but Sadie saw with a wave of relief that her chest was slowly moving up and down.

"Annie," Sadie whispered.

"Very good, Agent Price," Teddy said. "See anyone else you recognize?" His eyes flickered to the right of her, back toward the entrance. Sadie turned her head painfully and saw, with a shock, an unconscious Detective Boyd a few feet in the other direction from the fish. He was slumped over on himself, but she could hear his breath wheezing in his chest. It didn't sound good; in fact, he sounded as though he was on the verge of a serious asthma attack.

Then she saw the puddle of blood at his feet and the stain of it on his side. "You shot him," Sadie said, her voice sounding dull and heavy, as though it was coming from far away. Her vision blurred again, and she realized she had concussion. She took a few deep, slow breaths, willing her head to clear. She needed to keep her wits about her if she was to stand a chance of getting out of this. Although even she had to admit that her chances were looking like zero to none.

If she could just keep him talking…surely, when she, O'Hara, and Boyd didn't turn up, Linden would think to follow her? She just had to hope the detective spotted the roof of the outhouse. And soon. She laid her head back against the wall, willing the throbbing to stop even as the room spun around her. She closed her eyes.

"How did Boyd know it was you?" she asked. "Surely, he didn't figure it out by himself?"

She hadn't worded that right, she thought. She needed to flatter him and point out his cleverness, not remind him that a plodder like Boyd had caught him out. But even thinking was hurting.

"He's a snooper," Teddy said, sounding angry as she had guessed he would be. "I saw him from the window when I got back, sniffing around the outhouse. I don't know what tipped him off. It wasn't you, Ms. Hotshot," he laughed. "*You* thought it was *him*."

"Which you encouraged," Sadie said wearily. "This morning, you told me about Boyd's suspension on purpose. But why did you defend him when I told you students had complained?"

"Well, I couldn't make it look too obvious that I was trying to frame him," Teddy said reasonably. "Especially as I knew that you would go back and question him. But whoever complained about him did the trick, didn't they, throwing the spotlight onto him? After all, I had to make sure it wasn't on me. I knew Westwood would have an alibi."

"Westwood?" Sadie struggled to gather her thoughts. His arrest might have made the news by now, but it would be for the attempted rape, not the murders.

"It occurred to me once I saw the rental car place had a Jaguar like his." Teddy nodded. He looked relaxed on his barrel, happy to tell her about his schemes. She needed a way to distract him. Boyd's gun was still in its holster, but it wasn't going to be easy getting to it, not with her hands and feet shackled. Or her head feeling like a herd of elephants was stampeding inside it.

"What occurred to you? To frame him? Why Westwood?" Sadie was struggling to make sense of what he was telling her.

"I used to work for him," Teddy said. "Until about a year ago, then I took the job at the college. It doesn't pay as well, but it's better than working for that pervert." His face twisted with disgust, which would have been comical if it wasn't so horrific. Teddy was insane, she realized. He really thought Westwood was somehow so much more immoral than he was. Because he didn't rape his victims? Sadie tried not to show her revulsion, instead nodding slowly.

"Yeah. He's a piece of work."

"I saw him," Teddy spat. "Picking up young girls, bringing them back. Heard the things he was doing to them. He films them, you know that? It's disgusting. But the girls, they're just as bad. Following him around like idiots, all wide-eyed and moronic. *Look at me, Mr. Westwood, do it to me*. They deserve everything they get."

Sadie could hear the hatred in his voice. She had been right about the misogyny part, at least.

"So, you set him up?"

"It wasn't a big deal." Teddy shrugged. "But when I saw the car…well, I figured if I got seen, it wouldn't hurt to try and transfer any recognition. We're a similar build, so it was just a case of getting similar glasses and a jacket. He always dresses that way when he picks his dates up."

Sadie opened her eyes again and looked at him. She was tired, too tired to play this game with him, and no one was coming. But she had to keep fighting. "Why do you do it?" she said bluntly. "Why kill them the way you do?"

Teddy looked surprised for a moment but then gave her a slow smile. He stood up, keeping the gun on her as he walked over to the table where Annie Tyler was tied down. He picked up a filet knife that was lying on the table next to her and trailed the tip of it slowly across Annie's stomach, smiling dreamily at Sadie as he did so.

"I've never had anyone watch before," he said. "I think I like it."

He licked his lips, and there was an unmistakable swelling in the front of his pants. Sadie turned her head away in disgust. She might have been right about the misogyny, but she had been wrong about there being no overt sexual element to the kills. His arousal was obvious, his voice as low and intimate as though he was talking to a lover.

"You don't want to watch?" He sounded almost petulant. Swallowing, Sadie forced herself to turn her head back.

"You don't have to do this," she said quietly. "There's no way you can get away with all of this, not now. Four bodies? If you hand yourself in now, I can push to cut you a deal."

He shook his head at her, disappointed. "I can't stop now," he said. "It's too late." He sounded almost forlorn for a moment, then resumed trailing the knife across Annie's stomach. "This one was a fighter," he said, sounding proud.

He was too far gone to reason with. Sadie looked around while he was distracted, judging the distances either side of her. While still pointing roughly at her, his attention wasn't on his shotgun but on Annie. It could buy her a few seconds…

But what if he used those few seconds to plunge the knife into Annie's stomach?

"She looks like my first, you know," Teddy continued, lost in his murderous reverie.

"Roxie?"

Teddy shook his head again, impatient at her for not understanding. "No, my first girlfriend. I didn't kill her, but I wanted to. I wish I had. She was a whore," he spat, his mood changing in an instant as his face twisted in anger.

"What did she do to you?" Sadie tried to sound sympathetic, inching her way as imperviously as she could along the wall toward Detective Boyd. The shotgun had moved a little more off-target. Maybe another second of time.

"Do? She didn't do anything. She just lay there, all wide-eyed, with her mouth open. Like a dead fish. Then she told everyone that *I* couldn't satisfy *her*." His face burned with remembered humiliation.

Sadie shifted slightly onto her side, her body poised. "So, every girl you have killed, they have all been her, haven't they?" Sadie said, sounding bored. "The substitute girlfriend who killed your hard-on. You know that's Serial Killer 101, right? You couldn't even be original?"

He whirled around to face her fully, dropping the knife and grabbing the shotgun with both hands. Sadie kicked out with her shackled feet and hit her target. The bucket tipped over, sending fish and brine all over the floor between them. Teddy roared in anger and a bullet whizzed by her ear even as she tried to propel herself toward Boyd, crawling on her elbows, her cuffed hands reaching clumsily for his holster.

She wasn't going to make it. The next bullet would get her.

But Teddy was angry, and he ran at her in fury as he fired his next shot, which caused him to slip straight in the spilled brine, landing heavily on his back. His bullet slammed into the corrugated roof of the outhouse as Sadie's fingertips brushed Boyd's gun. As she fumbled with it, she could hear Teddy struggling to right himself, slipping and sliding in the brine as he tried to swing the shotgun back around toward her.

He had her in his sights again just as Sadie got the gun loose, rolled on her side, and aimed it at him.

They fired at the same time.

And then once again, everything went black.

CHAPTER TWENTY SEVEN

"Sadie? Sadie?" Someone was shaking her. She opened her eyes, yawned, and sat up, pushing her long hair out of her eyes. It was Jessica, sitting on the end of her bed.

"Come on, get dressed," her sister urged. "We're going to see Mom in the hospital again. Dad said she's coming home tomorrow."

Sadie stared at her sister. Two years older, Jessica was the prettier, smarter one. And the best-behaved. Sadie was sure that her parents loved Jessica more than her but that was okay, because she loved Jessica too, more than any person in the world ever. Since Mom had been ill, Jessica had taken good care of her, especially as their father was either at the hospital or at the saloon. His drinking was getting worse and worse since Mom had been sick.

"How long for?" Sadie asked, excited at the thought of their mother being home, but trying not to show it because she knew it wouldn't last. Mom would go back to the hospital again like she always did.

Or worse.

Sadie wasn't stupid. Although no one would come right out and say it, and any adult that she posed the question to avoided answering her, she knew that her mother was dying. That she was really, really sick, and when people were that sick, even the doctors couldn't make them better. If their mother was coming home, then it wasn't to get well.

Jessica's face fell as a shadow crossed it. She knew, too, but she wouldn't say it either. Instead, she took her little sister's hand. "I don't know," she said, her voice quivering as though she was the baby sister, not Sadie. "But at least we will have her back for a while. Now come on, or Dad will get mad."

Sadie pulled a face at her sister. "So? He's always mad. Or drunk. Or mad and drunk!" Sadie raised her voice and Jessica shushed her and looked anxiously over the edge of their balcony in case their father was in the cabin below. But the door was open, and they could hear him stamping around impatiently outside.

"Come on, I'll braid your hair. It will look pretty," Jessica pleaded. Sadie couldn't refuse her sister anything, and so she turned around and let her start brushing and threading her fingers through her hair, enjoying the brief moments before their father would start hollering at them or worse. These days, just looking at the girls—especially Sadie—seemed to agitate him. Sadie thought maybe if he didn't spend so much time at the saloon then he might be in a better mood, but even she didn't have the courage to say that to him.

"We have to take those pictures we drew for Mom," she said.

"We will. I put them in my backpack already," Jessica said. She was always organized, always tidy, unlike Sadie, who seemed to attract chaos. Their mother found that funny, whereas to their father it was just one in a long line of things to yell at her for, or worse, use the belt. That had only started since Mom had been in the hospital.

Sadie hoped she stayed home for a while. Before she…. had to go away. And then maybe things could be like old times, just for a while, with her and Jessica and their mother curled up on the couch in front of the fire, Mom telling them Inuit stories that she had heard from the village, about ghostly bears that haunted the mountains and the little people that lived in the caves. Sadie loved her mother's stories.

Yes, she was looking forward to seeing her.

Except, after that day, Sadie couldn't remember seeing her mother ever again.

*

"Agent Price? You still with us?"

It was Linden, peering over her, his face creased with concern. Sadie blinked, pulling herself out of her reverie. As she had suspected, she had a concussion, and she kept slipping into a half sleep, filled with half memories and flashbacks of Teddy standing over Annie Tyler's body. Shivering, she clasped her hands tighter around the hot cocoa someone had handed her.

They were in the ER at Anchorage's main hospital, not an unfamiliar place to her these last few months, and after being brought in half-conscious on a stretcher, she was eager to be told she could go home. She wanted her bed, and a deep, long sleep without dreams or memories.

But that last memory…that was important. That mattered. She filed it away, ready to examine when this was all over, and she could get back to that cave.

"Where's O'Hara?" she said instead.

Linden sat opposite her. “He’s going to be fine,” he reassured her. “He’s just sleeping off a huge dose of sedatives. Same as Annie Tyler. You rescued her, Agent Price. You got to her in time. I was thirty minutes behind you. You would have all been dead.” He sounded matter of fact rather than self-incriminatory, and Sadie understood that he was simply praising her. She smiled at him weakly.

“Thank you,” she said weakly.

Linden shrugged. “It’s just the truth.” His voice was gruff, almost embarrassed. Sadie took a sip of her cocoa, grateful for the warmth that filled her. “What about Teddy? And Detective Boyd?”

“Teddy’s dead. You got him at point-blank range in the chest. He didn’t hit you once, in spite of all the bullets peppering holes in that outhouse. You must have nine lives, Agent. I can’t say I’ve ever worked with anyone quite like you.”

Sadie decided to take that at face value and not try to work out whether it was intended as more insult or compliment.

“Detective Boyd is in surgery,” Linden went on. “HIs prognosis is good, although he’ll be laid up for a while. And I will be having a serious talk with him about charging off to check out Teddy without taking anyone with him. The job’s getting to him.”

Well, at least it wasn’t me this time, Sadie thought, remembering previous cases and her penchant for going off investigating alone. Something that both Cooper and Golightly had regularly chewed her out for.

Right on cue, Golightly walked into the room and came straight over to them, his eyes sweeping over Sadie. “Well, you look better than the last few times I’ve visited you here,” he told her.

“Yeah,” Sadie quipped, “so don’t worry, I won’t be needing any time off.”

“You can take tomorrow off at least,” he said firmly, like a father telling off a wayward child. Then he grinned at her. “You’re getting pretty good at this, Price. It’s about time you were honored for it. I’ve recommended you be put forward for a commendation.”

Sadie swallowed against sudden and uncharacteristic tears. “Thanks,” she murmured, not sure what to say. Or if it would even be allowed to happen if Internal Investigations was about to strip her of her badge.

Now that the case was over, she had to deal with the rest of her crazy, screwed-up life.

"You brought Westwood in as well," Detective Linden chimed in. "We have to thank you for that. I've got some updates for you that you might want to hear."

"Oh?"

Linden nodded. "Two other women have come forward and accused him of rape. Including the maid. I'm heading up a new major investigation into the creep; he's going down for a very long time if I've got anything to do with it. So—well done."

"Thanks," she said again, feeling overwhelmed by all the praise, especially from Detective Linden. She was glad to hear about Westwood, though, and suspected that Linden would find a lot of satisfaction from taking him down. She was about to say something else, but Linden lifted a hand in farewell and started to walk off.

"Hey, Detective," she called after him. He looked back over his shoulder at her. "I hope we can work together again soon." She grinned.

Linden barked out a laugh and looked almost sheepish before he walked away. Golightly grinned at Sadie. "I was worried you two would come to blows. Linden is pretty set in his ways."

"Yeah, he is. But he's a good detective." Sadie shifted uncomfortably in her seat, wondering when the nurse would turn up to give her the all-clear to go home. It was late evening now and she wanted nothing more than some food and then a good, long sleep.

"Got some things to tell you," Golightly said after a pause. "You want the bad news or the good news first?"

Sadie gave a heavy sigh, wondering if she was ever going to get a break or if life was going to endlessly continue to throw one challenge after another at her.

"Hit me with the bad news," she told him. "Might as well get it out of the way."

"I need you in my office first thing in the morning."

Sadie glared at him. "What happened to the day off?"

"You can have it. But I'm expecting a call from Quantico in the morning. With the decision on your case from Internal Investigations."

It felt like a sucker punch to the stomach as Sadie sucked in a deep breath. She hadn't had much of a conversation with Golightly about the whole affair. Her boss was a man of a few words and not one to pry into matters unless he needed to, which Sadie, as an intensely private person, appreciated. But they both knew that if the decision was unfavorable then Sadie would be doing a lot more tomorrow than having one day off.

She would be handing in her badge.

And then what would she do? Become a security guard, like Detective Boyd? Be a private detective of some description? She couldn't think of much worse, but what else could she do? She had never thought beyond a life in the FBI. She had gone to Quantico straight out of college and never considered doing anything else. Not until the Mangler.

Maybe she would give it all up. Escape into the wilds of Alaska and become a trapper or an ice fisherman. Or help Caz behind the bar at the saloon. Maybe a quieter life wouldn't be so bad. She had her father's cabin, too, still sitting there untouched since he had died just last month. Caz hadn't asked her to move out of her room above the saloon garage, so Sadie had ignored the place, having no desire to go back there.

She rubbed a hand across her face. She was exhausted and aching and in no position to even start thinking about major life decisions.

"You okay, Price? I'm hoping it won't be bad news. I've been updating Quantico on all your successes since you got here. You're my best agent and I don't want to lose you."

Sadie tried to articulate another "thank you," but felt that she would burst into tears if she spoke. Refusing to cry in front of her boss, she took a long drink of her cocoa instead.

"Okay," she said as she drained her cup. The nurse was walking over to them. "What's the good news?"

"I picked Sheriff Cooper up and brought him over with me. He'll drive you back in your truck. You don't want to be driving yourself with that concussion."

Sadie frowned at him. "That's it?"

Golightly gave her a grin that made her cheeks go warm. "Well, I thought you would be pleased to see him."

Sadie didn't answer, relieved to see that the nurse had reached them. *Jesus,* she thought. Did everyone know what was bubbling between her and Cooper? She thought they had been discreet.

"You're free to go," the nurse told Sadie cheerfully. "You've got a ride home?"

"Yes," Sadie confirmed, ignoring Golightly's grin. She didn't think she had ever seen her boss smile so much. She stood up, crumpled her cup, and tossed it into the trash. “Let’s go,” she said to no one in particular.

She walked out into the evening darkness, a light flurry of snow looking like falling blossoms in the lights of the truck. Golightly disappeared across the parking lot, leaving Sadie to walk toward the truck, watching Cooper’s silhouette in the driver’s seat. For a moment, her heart leaped in her chest.

Play it cool, Price, she told herself. It had been a kiss, nothing more.

But as the door swung open and she climbed into the passenger seat, the sight of Cooper’s warm, smiling eyes prompted a smile that nearly split her cheeks.

“Hey,” she said softly.

“Hey,” he said. He reached out and stroked a finger down the side of her jaw. “You’re less beat up than the last time, at least.”

“Golightly said something similar,” Sadie laughed. Then Cooper suddenly pulled her into a bear hug. Sadie laid her head on his shoulder, allowing herself, just for a moment, to let go of all the tension. All the worries. To feel safe from the outside world and her own demons for just a few blissful moments.

“Goddammit, Price,” Cooper murmured into her hair. “You’ve got to stop getting yourself into trouble like this.” He pulled away but kept an arm around her shoulders. “Are you okay? Golightly only gave me bare facts, but it sounds pretty scary.”

“It was,” Sadie admitted. “This guy was one sick puppy.”

“I meant having to work with Linden,” Cooper said with a grin, and Sadie laughed, feeling the aches leaving her body. How had it come to this? Not so long ago Cooper had been able to infuriate her more than anyone, and now she was craving his company like a kid for sweets.

She had to stop this; a warning voice came from somewhere in the recesses of her mind. Old defense systems that she had built up a very long time ago. Loving people was dangerous. It got you hurt, and heartbroken.

Especially when you couldn’t save them.

But as Cooper gazed into her eyes, she forced her fears away. They could keep, too. She had also learned a long time ago that if you didn’t keep things in the day then wondering about the future and the past could crush you. Maybe, soon, she would have to think about what was really going on between her and the sheriff and decide what the hell she was going to do about it.

But not today. Not tonight. After everything that had just happened, and everything she knew she still had to face over the next few days, she wanted—no, needed—to throw caution to the wind for just one night.

She leaned in and kissed him, the electricity igniting between them the minute their lips touched. He ran his hands through her hair, pulling her to him with a low groan coming deep from his throat.

"Cooper," she said, against his mouth. "Take me back to your place tonight?"

His eyes went wide and wondering. "You're sure?" he whispered.

Sadie kissed him again.

"Yes," she said, "I'm sure."

CHAPTER TWENTY EIGHT

Sadie could hear Golightly's voice inside the office, clearly on a phone call, and wondered if it was to Internal Investigations or if he had already spoken to them.

She was sitting in the outer office of the ASAC at the Field Office for Anchorage FBI. Technically she had her own office here now, but she had never had the chance to use it. Most of her cases since she had arrived had taken her into the hinterlands on the outskirts of Anchorage, near her own hometown, and the case she had first worked with O'Hara had taken them all the way up into the darkness of the north and the Beaufort Sea.

This was the first time, in fact, that she had actually worked a case in Anchorage proper, and she had spent all of her time at the APD station. It had been pleasant to arrive at the field office that morning and sit at her own desk to write up her notes on the Teddy case.

It would have been a lot more pleasant if she hadn't also spent the time waiting to be summoned to see Golightly. If she already knew whether she still had her badge or not. She'd never been the most patient of people, and the suspense was eating away at her gut.

It had hit her as soon as she had opened her eyes that morning. No, she corrected her own thoughts, it had been the second thing that had hit her. The first had been the fact that she wasn't in her own bed, and that Cooper was next to her.

In spite of her angst, Sadie couldn't help but smile to herself as she remembered the way he had turned his head on his pillow, opened his eyes, and blinked in surprise to see her, then smiled that slow, sexy smile of his as he too remembered the night before.

They hadn't spoken about what it meant, or what the future held, but he had kissed her as she got into her truck and told her to call him when she was done.

"Are you busy today?" she had asked, and then, before he thought she was asking for a date, "I want to go back to the cave."

"Already? Don't you want to wait and see what Golightly says?"

But Sadie had shaken her head, as stubborn as ever. She might as well get all of the bad news out of the way together. Whatever awaited her in that cave, it wasn't going to be good.

She had also managed to convince herself that Golightly was going to be asking for her badge. Recalling the meeting that she had in his office with Internal Investigations before the Beaufort case, she knew that the lead investigator hadn't believed a word that Sadie had said. Had thought that Sadie had acted with excessive force. That the Mangler hadn't needed to die.

Sadie sat on her hands as she realized they were shaking. Those last moments with the Mangler were ones that Sadie had erased from her consciousness as best she could. It was the first time in her career that she had been genuinely terrified for her life.

That she had thought that she was going to die at the hands of one of the most sadistic serial killers that America had ever known. In all the cases since, no matter how sticky the situation, Sadie had never experienced that same gut-churning terror.

Could she really say that she had needed to shoot him after hitting him on the head with the length of rebar? And shoot him right in his heart? It was a killing shot, and he was already falling to the floor.

Or was he on the floor?

The truth was, in spite of the calm and logical account that Sadie had given in the investigation, her memories were still blurred with shock. She had a very crystal-clear image of raising her gun, and in a single split second, knowing that she was shooting to kill. But was that only to stop him killing her, or because she thought that he deserved to die? Sometimes, in the very dead of night, Sadie wasn't so certain of the answer.

Life wasn't as black and white as Internal Investigations wanted it to be, and sometimes those split-second decisions were messy and driven by instinct rather than logic. Most of the time, Sadie knew she hadn't done anything wrong.

She was no coldblooded killer. She was the one who hunted them.

But in her worst moments, she wondered if they were right, and if sometimes the hunt could turn you into something like the monster you were hunting.

She felt a familiar panic rise in her throat, the same feeling that she got in her nightmares, and she shook her head and took a deep breath to clear it, willing herself back into the present. Concentrating on her surroundings. The almost threadbare carpet. The clock ticking, too loudly, on the wall.

"Agent Price?" Golightly's secretary poked her head out of the door.

Sadie stood up, put on a carefully neutral expression, and walked through the now open door. The secretary left, leaving her with Golightly, who waved her into the seat opposite his desk. His office was as messy as ever.

"Price. How are you feeling after yesterday?"

"Good, sir. A bit of a headache, but nothing major. Has Agent O'Hara come around?"

"Yes." Golightly nodded, looking relieved. "He will be on his way home by now. I gave him a few days off. This is the first time something like this has happened to him. I told him to get used to it. Especially if he keeps partnering with you."

"I'll drop by and check on him," Sadie said with a smile at Golightly's joke.

There was an awkward silence, and then Golightly cleared his throat. *Here we go*, Sadie thought. Her stomach twisted at the thought of having to hand her badge in. Everything she had worked so hard for, gone.

"The investigation has been closed, Price," he said.

Sadie stared at him. What did that mean? "They came to a decision?"

"Yeah," Golightly said. "That they were wasting their time, which was exactly what I told them. Nothing to investigate. You're in the clear, Price."

He said it so matter-of-factly, as though there had never been any doubt, that Sadie didn't quite know how to react. Golightly continued talking, as though he hadn't just given her the best news she had heard in months.

"I personally don't think there ever was a case against you," the ASAC said, "but there's no doubt your recent successes have helped, too. I bet they thought you would disappear into obscurity up here," he chuckled.

"I… I don't know what to say," Sadie said, shaking her head. "I was preparing myself for the exact opposite."

Golightly shook his head. "Not like you to give up so easy, Price. They can't afford to get rid of you. You're one of our best agents and have taken down too many high-profile killers recently. They don't want to be seen to be letting go of their star special agent. You're a national hero for getting rid of the Mangler, I was shocked they even opened the investigation, quite frankly."

"Too much of a high-profile case not to," Sadie said, sounding and feeling dazed. "Although I suppose it could work both ways. Honestly, I had prepared myself to be handing my badge in."

"Well, you're not," Golightly said briskly. "So don't be resting on your laurels just yet. If you want it, there's a promotion for you. Thanks to this recent crime wave Quantico has finally listened to me about needing more agents and more funding."

Sadie, still absorbing the news, was struggling to keep up with Golightly's change of topic. One word stood out, though.

"Promotion?"

Looking pleased, Golightly steepled his fingers together on his desk and regarded her for a moment before nodding. "Yes. We have a position opening up for a senior field agent, and there is no one better qualified than you to take it. What do you say? It will a mean substantial pay increase, an office almost as nice as this one, and you will be my operational lieutenant. It's a good career jump, Price."

Sadie sat back in her chair feeling slightly blown away. It would be an excellent career progression, especially when she hadn't yet turned thirty.

"Well, don't bite my hand off, Price," Golightly said, raising an eyebrow. He had obviously expected her to be thrilled, and she was.

Kind of.

"I'm incredibly grateful, sir," she began, not sure how to explain her reticence. Golightly had no idea that she was investigating her sister's cold case with Cooper.

"There's a 'but' coming."

"It's just, I suppose I had never planned on coming back to Alaska permanently. And since my father's death…"

"I understand," Golightly said. "There's nothing to keep you here?"

That wasn't it, Sadie realized. There was more to keep her here than there had ever been. She had hated her father. His abuse and Jessica's murder had been the reason she had left while still a teenager. Then she had come back after the Mangler case, needing to get away from the aftermath of the case and the impending investigation, and also knowing that it was way past time that she found out what had really happened to Jessica. But she had never planned on staying.

But now she had friends. Jane Cooper, Caz, and little Jenny, and colleagues she cared about like O'Hara. She had a community.

And—although she inwardly winced at admitting it to herself—she had even fallen in love.

The new job offer should be the icing on the cake.

But she knew, now that the last case was over and the investigation had been dropped, that she couldn't make any more decisions about her future until she found out what had happened to her family.

Because it wasn't just Jessica's murder, she was now investigating but the potential disappearance of her mother. And the fact that her father seemed to have known something about both. Whatever she was about to discover, she knew it could blow her world wide open. She couldn't commit to anything until she knew.

But she couldn't tell Golightly about all of that.

"I want to take it," she said to Golightly. "But there are a few personal things regarding my father's death that have come to light. I really need to get those sorted before I can make a commitment like that."

"Anything I can do to help?" Golightly asked, looking sympathetic.

Sadie shook her head. "No, just give me some time to sort it out before I can give you an answer?"

Golightly looked disappointed but nodded. "Okay, Price. I can hold it open for a couple of weeks, tops."

"Thank you, sir."

Sadie left the office and walked through the building, emerging into the bright, cold sunshine. It was a new day, and after last night and this morning, everything had suddenly changed.

She had the chance of a future again.

But first, she had to confront the ghosts of the past.

CHAPTER TWENTY NINE

Cooper met her on the porch of her father's old cabin. For some reason she hadn't wanted to go in on her own. A month after he had died, it felt as though it was both years ago and as though he was still here, his malevolent presence curled around the place like an aura.

Cooper paused at the bottom of the porch, his eyes searching her face. "How did it go with Golightly?"

"I've been cleared." In spite of where they were, she couldn't help smiling. Even more so when Cooper bounded up onto the porch and grabbed her in a bear hug.

"I knew it. They would be nuts to let you go. I bet Golightly was happy."

"He was." She decided not to tell him about the offer of a promotion, not yet. Not until this was over.

She had to wonder if it would ever be over, if the mystery would ever be solved. She had sworn years ago that one day she would get justice for Jessica, but she could never have expected that her entire family would end up being dragged into it. So far, she had more questions than answers.

"I brought the file on your mother," Cooper said quietly, handing it over. "There's literally nothing to it, just a missing person's report from your father."

Sadie flipped through it, a pang of grief stabbing her as she had a vivid recollection of her mother before she got sick, stroking Sadie's hair as she went to sleep.

"He must have killed her," she whispered. "And decided he had to confess before he died. But why? She was dying anyway."

"Do you know how long she had?"

Sadie shook her head. "No. Depending on what we find in the cave, I'm going to ask for her medical records."

"I was wondering…assuming anyone did kill her, which we don't know…could it have been a mercy killing, by your father? I mean, he did love her, right?"

Sadie felt a wave of hatred for him, and a reluctance to believe that he could do anything that compassionate, however misguided, but she had to concede that it was as good a theory as any.

"The thing I don't understand," she said in frustration, "is why, when the last time we spoke I was asking him to tell me the truth about Jessica, he would leave me with some kind of confession about my mother? Although in a way it is just like the contrary old sonofabitch," she said with a sigh. "Instead of answering one mystery, he just leaves me with another."

Cooper laid a hand on her arm. "We're gonna figure it out," he reassured her. "Do you remember anything that might relate, now that you know about the missing person's report?"

Sadie remembered her flashback in the ER.

"Yeah," she said quietly. "I remember the last time I saw my mom in the hospital. I was with Jessica, and Mom was so happy to see us…" She paused, willing herself not to cry. Not yet, not until she knew exactly what it was that she was grieving.

"Go on," Cooper said softly.

"I've always assumed that was the last time I saw her because she died soon after. I remember she was so thin, so ill…. But then yesterday, I remembered Jessica that morning, saying that Mom was coming home soon. Coming home to die, I guess, but coming home. Only she never did. And Dad just told us she had died. But that morning…. she didn't seem at death's door, you know? She was looking forward to being home."

Sadie shook her head in frustration, wiping sudden, hot tears from her cheeks savagely with the back of her hand. "But I don't know if my memory is just playing tricks on me because of what I've just discovered," she admitted. "I mean, I was seven, Cooper, you know?"

"I know," Cooper said in a soft voice. Sadie resisted the urge to throw herself into his arms, instead squaring her shoulders back and lifting her chin.

"Let's go in." She took the key out from her pocket.

The cabin smelled dusty and had the chill of an empty house that hadn't known warmth for some time. The ashes of her father's last fire were still in the grate and an empty coffee cup sat on the table. The place was different from how it had looked while she was growing up; even sparser, if that was possible, and at some point, he had decorated, although it was old and faded now. Still, the layout was family, and she had a vision of herself and Jessica playing as she looked up at their old balcony. She swallowed the lump in her throat.

"Where do you want to start?" Cooper asked.

"I'm not sure there's anywhere to start from," Sadie said as she looked around. "He wasn't exactly a hoarder. Maybe in the pantry where he used to keep his hunting gear." She walked through the kitchen to the walk-in cupboard at the back behind a moth-eaten curtain. Her father's hunting gear was there, including his guns.

He had threatened to shoot her, once. She had been thirteen. It had been Jessica, as ever, who got in between them.

"There's something on that shelf." Cooper pointed. "It looks like a keepsake box."

It was too high for Sadie to reach, so Cooper lifted it down for her. With a jolt, Sadie recognized the small wooden box with its flowery carvings.

"This was my mother's," she said, stroking the lid. "She was given it by an Inuit guy. She helped his wife in labor when the snow was too bad to get her to the hospital. Saved the baby's life. He was a carpenter, and he made this especially for her."

"She sounds like a much-loved woman," Cooper said. "And maybe someone in the Inuit village would know more about all this? And about those letters?"

"Mother Dawn," Sadie said quietly, remembering the marks on the map that they had overlooked at first.

Holding her breath, Sadie opened the box. There were baby photos of her and Jessica on top, followed by wedding photos of her and her father.

"My God, he actually looks happy for once," she said, running her fingers over the pictures. "I guess this was before he started drinking."

"He was a drunk before your mother got sick?" Cooper asked.

Sadie nodded. "I don't remember him ever not being a mean bastard," she said. "He just got worse after that."

"How about after Jessica…died?"

Sadie frowned as she remembered. "I was fifteen then. He couldn't really beat me anymore—I had started fighting back, and I could fight even then. I used to go into Anchorage and do self-defense at the gym. We just kind of ignored each other all the way until I left for college."

Cooper stood behind her and squeezed her shoulders. "That must have been lonely."

"It was," she admitted. "I had friends, and a boyfriend… But how could anyone understand, really? I couldn't wait to get out of here. I didn't come back until last December, when I met you."

Did you have any contact with your dad? I mean, did he never say anything about what happened to Jessica or your mom?"

"We didn't keep in contact," Sadie said. "The day I said I was leaving, and that I wanted to go into the FBI, he told me if I was going to never come back. That he didn't want to see me again. I took him at his word."

She could feel Cooper looking at her and she started burrowing into the box again. She didn't want to see the pity on his face. There were thank you letters and cards from patients, and pictures of babies that her mother had delivered. On closer inspection, Sadie realized something.

"These are all from her Inuit patients," she said, reading a letter from a mother whose twins Sadie's mom had delivered. "It seems she had a lot more work with them than I ever knew…she seems to have been something like a community midwife for them. It says here, she even trained with an Inuit doula."

"She must have been quite something," Cooper said, reading over her shoulder. "The residents in the village tend to keep themselves to themselves, so for an outsider to be so loved is quite unusual. She seems to have almost been adopted into the community."

"Look at this one," Sadie said as a phrase jumped out at her. "It's addressed to 'Mother Dawn.' It's like a name they've given to her."

"The same name your father wrote in Inuit on the back of his map," Cooper said slowly. "So, he wasn't just saying 'your mother, Dawn.' He was directly referring to her Inuit moniker, and her work with them."

"But why?" Sadie felt more confused than ever. "What can her midwifery practice have to do with her disappearing? Do you think…she went to the village to die, or something?"

Cooper frowned. "But why cover it up for so long? And why file a missing person's report? The village doesn't like any outside interference from the law either. Remember that first case we worked together? I can't see them harboring her in secret, especially if it didn't need to be a secret. It makes no sense," he added, sounding almost as frustrated as Sadie felt.

"No, it doesn't." Sadie replaced the letters, closed the box tenderly, and then put it into her backpack. She didn't want anything else from the cabin, but this was coming with her. All those years and she hadn't even known it had existed, and her father had deprived her of the pictures of her mother and sister, as well as valuable knowledge that would have helped her know more about the woman her mother was. For a while after he had died, Sadie had thought that her resentments had died with him, but now they were flaring to life again.

Especially when she couldn't ignore the possibility that he had killed one or both of them.

"I need to go inside that cave, Cooper," she said quietly.

"Are you sure you want to do it today? You've had a wild couple of days." He turned her to face him and searched her face, his eyes full of such concern that she wanted to cry again.

I'm getting soft, she thought. *Coming home has turned me into a cry baby.* But there was something about Cooper that made her feel safe with him. As though it was okay to be vulnerable.

"I have to," she said.

"Okay." Cooper took her hand. "Then let's do this."

As they left the cabin and Sadie locked up, she felt dread growing in her chest as she wondered what they were about to find. More clues? More maps? It wouldn't entirely surprise her if her father had sent her off on a wild goose chase. One last attempt to make her life a misery.

Or maybe he really was trying to tell her something important.

Tell her, or finally confess? She didn't even want to think about the potential emotional impact. For a brief second, she wondered if she wouldn't be better off just forgetting all this and letting her family rest. She knew well enough that some cases were never solved, and some families just had to live with not knowing. That sometimes being spared the details was a kindness.

But she also knew that couldn't be her. For nearly fifteen years she had been promising her sister justice, and if turned out that the whole thing was even bigger than she could have dreamed, then so be it. She hadn't become an FBI hotshot by burying her head in the sand and not taking risks.

"Yeah," she said, echoing Cooper's earlier words. "Let's do this."

CHAPTER THIRTY

Sadie was silent on the drive back to the headwaters of the river, just as she had been a few days before on their first trip out here when they had found the cave. Then, it had been a loud silence; wired and buzzing with anticipation. Now, it felt heavy and full of foreboding.

"Whatever we find out here," Cooper said eventually as he drove his snowcat through the pine trees, "I'm here for you, Sadie. We'll figure this out."

Sadie reached out and touched the back of his hand by way of reply. There didn't seem to be anything more that needed to be said.

The pine trees gave way to a frozen tundra that remained ice in some places most of the year round, stretching on up to the smoky mountains, and she caught sight of the river. They were nearly at the rocky headwaters and the place where they had found the cave.

"It was pretty well hidden, that cave," she said. "I'm at a loss as to how my father even knew about it."

"He hunted, didn't he? Maybe he came across it."

"Maybe, but he didn't hunt any more than most of the guys around here. He wasn't an expert on the landscape, not like some of the trappers are."

"And many of the Inuit, especially from the village," Cooper pointed out.

Sadie nodded, staring out the window at where the rocky outcrop concealed the cave entrance as Cooper pulled up. She got out, tying her hair up into a tighter knot as she grabbed her Maglite and climbing ropes. They had no idea how far or deep the cave went, or even how safe it was, but she guessed that they were about to find out.

Cooper put an arm around her shoulders as they approached it, and she didn't resist but instead leaned into his body, absorbing his strength into her own.

"Here it is." Cooper ran his hand along the rock, finding the vertical ledge that became an entrance, just wide enough for one person at a time to squeeze into.

"I'll go first," Cooper said, as she had known he would, but Sadie laid a hand on his arm to stop him. "This isn't the time for your playing hero, Cooper," she said. "I need to be the first to see whatever it is that's in here."

Cooper took one look at her face and acquiesced, stepping back and letting her go ahead. Sadie squeezed herself into the gap, surprised at how quickly it widened out into a passage that led down on a steep incline. She shone her Maglite around and then gasped.

"Cooper, there's some rusty old rails at the sides. This cave has been used."

"Mining shaft," Cooper said as he came up behind her. "Be careful. Some of them are treacherous."

Sadie moved forward carefully, shining her Maglite with one hand, her other hand on the rail, which was icy enough that it stung her skin through her gloves. It was freezing in the cave, and she could see her breath, curling in the narrow beam of light coming from her Maglite. Any daylight coming from the narrow opening had disappeared quickly, and the only light was their own. Cooper kept his flashlight trained on the floor in front of them while Sadie kept hers ahead.

"Whoa," Cooper said quickly, grabbing her from behind. "There's an old mining shaft there."

Sadie looked down where his light was pointing and saw the old shaft. "This must go right back to gold rush days," she said wonderingly. It felt almost as though they were caught out of time. She shone her light straight down the shaft.

And her hand flew to her mouth as she gasped. "Damn," Cooper said behind her as he, too, stared down the shaft, which was about thirty feet deep.

At the bottom was a skeleton.

Skeletons weren't a rare find in some of the old gold mines, especially the more treacherous ones. Miners who had fallen and never been able to get back up, or who were even killed by fellow gold diggers looking to steal their findings, had been discovered and sometimes made local news. Especially if the remains turned out to be some long-lost ancestor of local families.

But this body wasn't that old. Faded clothing still clung to it, remnants of a dress that, while dusty and faded, looked relatively modern. There were still strands of long, dark hair on the skull.

Like Jessica's. Like their mother's. Sadie tasted bile in the back of her throat but swallowed it down, willing herself not to be sick.

"Female," Cooper said, his voice echoing down the shaft. "Quite petite. Could it be…?"

"It could be," Sadie said, her voice thick in her mouth. There suddenly didn't seem to be enough air inside the mine.

"It might not be, though," Cooper said. "There are a lot of bodies found in these places."

Sadie nodded. "Yeah. It could be anyone."

But she knew it wasn't.

"Help me with the ropes," she said to Cooper, passing them to him. "I need to go down."

Cooper looked as though he was about to protest and offer to go himself, but then he thought better of it. Silently, he helped her with the ropes, holding on as she rappelled down the narrow shaft and shining his Maglite ahead of her. She didn't look down until she was right near the bottom, only to ensure that she didn't step on the remains.

Landing softly, she crouched down next to the skeleton, holding her breath. Left here unembalmed, the body would have decomposed quickly. What was left of the dress didn't look like anything she recognized. The only way she was going to know who this was would be to take the bones away for testing. There wasn't enough left to identify.

Then Sadie noticed a small stone amulet around the collarbone, hanging forlornly against the chest bones. For a second, she felt a wave of relief. She had never seen her mother wear anything like this. It wasn't her.

But then she saw the engraving on the amulet and realized that it looked familiar, like something she had seen before. She leaned closer, her heart thumping in her chest as though it would burst out through her rib bones.

The amulet was engraved with two small symbols.

No, not symbols. Words.

Inuit words.

An anguished howl escaped Sadie's mouth as she realized what they said.

Mother Dawn.

NOW AVAILABLE!

<u>ONLY MADNESS</u>
(A Sadie Price FBI Suspense Thriller—Book 6)

Hitchhikers are turning up dead in the Alaskan wilderness, found near truck stops along empty stretches of highway. In a lonely, remote landscape, Sadie must comb the insular world of truckers to search for suspects. But, all alone out there, might Sadie find herself a victim?

ONLY MADNESS (A Sadie Price FBI Suspense Thriller) is book #6 in a chilling new series by mystery and thriller author Rylie Dark, which begins with ONLY MURDER (book #1).

Special Agent Sadie Price, a 29-year-old rising star in the FBI's BAU unit, stuns her colleagues by requesting reassignment to the FBI's remote Alaskan field office. Back in her home state, a place she vowed she would never return, Sadie, running from a secret in her recent past and back into her old one, finds herself facing her demons—including her sister's unsolved murder—while assigned to hunt down a new serial killer.

Sadie's investigation leads her into the Alaskan wasteland, full of bleak landscapes, hardened loners, and endless cold. As she fights to piece together the clues, Sadie finds herself in a race against time.

Can she stop the killer before another girl is taken?

An action-packed page-turner, the SADIE PRICE series is a riveting crime thriller, jammed with suspense, surprises and twists and turns that you won't see coming. It will have you fall in love with a brilliant and scarred new character, while challenging you, amidst a barren landscape, to solve an impenetrable crime.

Future books in the series will be available soon.

Rylie Dark

Bestselling author Rylie Dark is author of the SADIE PRICE FBI SUSPENSE THRILLER series, comprising six books (and counting); the MIA NORTH FBI SUSPENSE THRILLER series, comprising six books (and counting); the CARLY SEE FBI SUSPENSE THRILLER, comprising six books (and counting); and the MORGAN STARK FBI SUSPENSE THRILLER, comprising three books (and counting).

An avid reader and lifelong fan of the mystery and thriller genres, Rylie loves to hear from you, so please feel free to visit www.ryliedark.com to learn more and stay in touch.

BOOKS BY RYLIE DARK

SADIE PRICE FBI SUSPENSE THRILLER

ONLY MURDER (Book #1)
ONLY RAGE (Book #2)
ONLY HIS (Book #3)
ONLY ONCE (Book #4)
ONLY SPITE (Book #5)
ONLY MADNESS (Book #6)

MIA NORTH FBI SUSPENSE THRILLER

SEE HER RUN (Book #1)
SEE HER HIDE (Book #2)
SEE HER SCREAM (Book #3)
SEE HER VANISH (Book #4)
SEE HER GONE (Book #5)
SEE HER DEAD (Book #6)

CARLY SEE FBI SUSPENSE THRILLER

NO WAY OUT (Book #1)
NO WAY BACK (Book #2)
NO WAY HOME (Book #3)
NO WAY LEFT (Book #4)
NO WAY UP (Book #5)
NO WAY TO DIE (Book #6)

MORGAN STARK FBI SUSPENSE THRILLER

TOO LATE (Book #1)
TOO CLOSE (Book #2)
TOO FAR GONE (Book #3)

www.ingramcontent.com/pod-product-compliance
Lightning Source LLC
Chambersburg PA
CBHW030614310726
48979CB00003B/710

* 9 7 8 1 0 9 4 3 9 5 0 7 4 *